The Greatest Battle *of* Culture

PANIGRAHI BETHI

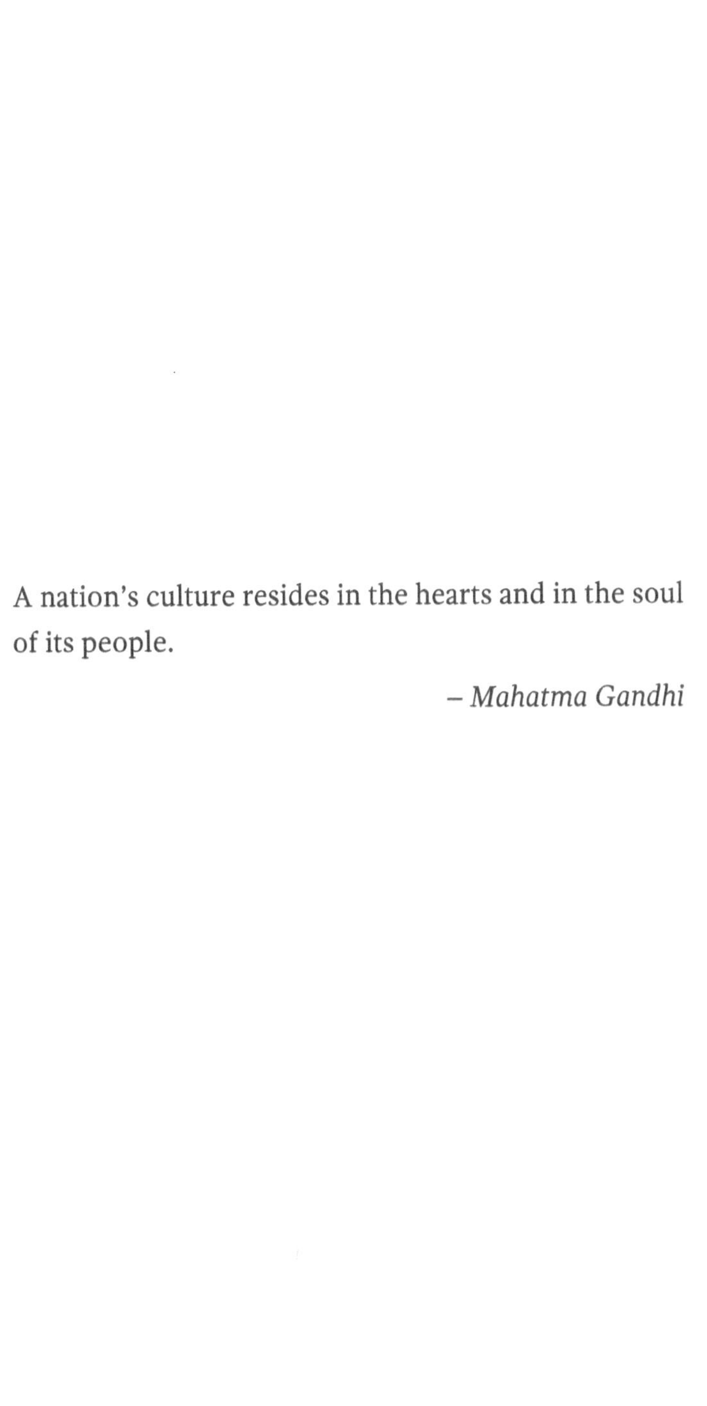

A nation's culture resides in the hearts and in the soul
of its people.

– *Mahatma Gandhi*

Contents

Prologue

Harappa, Indus Valley Region, 1500 BCE

As humans invented agriculture twelve thousand years ago, a civilization emerged along the banks of Sindhu River in the present-day Indian subcontinent. It came to be called the **Indus Valley Civilization**, and it grew like a giant sequoia tree over the several millennia. The people of Indus Valley were a great example of an advanced society with complex script and sophisticated culture.

Harappa and Mohenjo-Daro were two major cities that showcased the people's intelligence, with their thoughtful urban planning and underground drainage system. Its impressive architecture competed with the greatest cities of the ancient world.

The people of Indus Valley, also called Harappans, were a peace-loving community focusing on excelling at what they do. They lived in harmony with a strong sense of community. They were skilled at many things with a deep understanding of the soil and seasons. Harappa was a hub of activity, with traders from all over the region coming to exchange goods and share their stories.

Just as the Indus Valley Civilization was thriving with richness, a new group of nomadic people called Aryans, arrived with their Vedic literature and Sanskrit language. They migrated slowly with their tribal groups from the distant steppe lands in the north into different parts of the valley. This marked the beginning of a significant cultural encounter, one that made a profound impact on later generations of the subcontinent.

The Aryans were a male dominated society, with a strong emphasis on the family and clan, whereas the Harappans were more egalitarian, with women playing a significant role in society.

This epic story goes through many generations, tracing the conflicts and collaborations of Harappans and Aryans. As the story evolves, it reveals the emergence of new leaders and thinkers that would go on to shape the values, traditions, and religions of the people of India. On a high level, the story innately reveals how Hinduism evolved over the period.

Author's Note

This story is a work of fiction, inspired by ancient history and genome study of the Indus Valley people that was published by various scientists. While this story is based on major historical events, the characters in this story are fictional and not supposed to be taken as historical fact.

Now let's start our journey into the world of ancient India...

Chapter One

The Language of Power

The citadel of Harappa rose majestically, its mud-brick walls glowing with a warm, golden light. The city's vibrant energy resonated through the air into the distant valley. Intricate carvings and paintings adorned the architecture, depicting tigers, unicorns, and everyday life, making the city a beautiful center of activity. Two elegant stone elephants flanked the entrance, their wise and gentle faces guarding the gateway to the city's heart.

Above the entrance, the magnificent statue of the Mother Goddess stood tall, her serene face gazing out over the city with an air of nurturing protection. Her outstretched arms embraced the people and the valley, her lap overflowing with abundance - fruits, grains, and flowers. Her eyes shone with a gentle light, illuminating the path for all who lived within the city's walls.

As evening fell, the people of Harappa moved about the city with grace and purpose, their hair and skin aglow in the warm light of torches and lamps.

Men wore shortened version of dhotis, showing muscular arms and shoulders as evidence of their hard work and labor. Women wore long skirts in vibrant colors with silver ornaments twinkling like stars in the dark sky.

Children played in the streets with laughter and screams as they chased each other through the crowded marketplace. Some paused in their daily activities to worship the Mother Goddess with offerings of flowers, milk, and honey.

Meanwhile, the newly arrived Aryan community settled in the outskirts of Harappa. They were a nomadic people, their paths tracing the ancient rivers like veins on a map. Their culture was shaped by the fiery power of Agni (*fire*) and the thunder of Indra (*king of gods*), where warriors rode the horses and sacred hymns were sung to the gods. Priests and poets wove tales of heroes and gods, their words painting vivid pictures in the minds of their listeners, their stories a reflection of their beliefs and values.

As the Harappans went about their daily lives, Purusha, a young Aryan warrior, arrived at the

Harappan palace, his footsteps echoing like a drumbeat announcing the arrival of a new era.

He entered the grand courtyard with a confident stride, his piercing blue eyes scanning the scene before him like a conqueror claiming new territory.

The vibrant colors of the murals seemed to dance in the fading light, and the hum of activity - nobles and scholars hurrying about their business - filled the air like the buzzing of a hive. As a member of the Vedic tribe, Purusha was proud of his people's heritage and culture, which had allowed them to spread their influence across the land like a river flowing to the sea.

The Harappan Chief, Baguhara, a middle-aged ruler with a robust build and a deep compassion for his people and the territory he ruled, greeted Purusha with a warm smile that seemed to hold a hint of caution. His dark hair was flecked with grey, reflecting his years of wisdom and experience, and his eyes shone with a devotion to his kingdom that bordered on reverence.

"Ah, young Aryan, I see you've arrived with a message from your people," Baguhara said, his voice warm and inviting, like a gentle whisper on a searing afternoon. "I trust it brings a proposal for peace and trade?"

Purusha nodded, his face gleaming in the sunlight like polished copper. "Indeed, Your Majesty. My people wish to share our Vedic knowledge with your people, in exchange for access to your city's riches."

Baguhara's eyes narrowed, his brow furrowing like a field freshly plowed. "I don't think it's that simple, Purusha. Our cultures are vastly different, and our people have a long history of misunderstandings. What makes you think your Vedic knowledge will be accepted here?"

Purusha's smile wavered, and he moved uncomfortably in his seat, like a warrior adjusting his armor before the battle. "I don't mean any offense, Your Majesty. I simply believe that our two cultures could complement each other, and—"

Baguhara's hand shot up, his palm facing Purusha like a barrier. "Enough, Purusha. I have heard enough of your proposals. You may leave now and take your 'superior knowledge' with you."

Purusha's expression faltered, and he rose from his seat, his shoulders sagging in a moment of uncharacteristic humility, like a warrior defeated in the battle. "I apologize, Your Majesty. I did not mean to offend. I will leave and reconsider my approach."

Baguhara's expression softened slightly, like a cooling respite on a summer day. "See that you do,

Purusha. And perhaps next time, come with a more open mind and a willingness to listen."

With that, Purusha left the throne room, his head bowed in defeat, his pride wounded, and his confidence shaken. He realized that he had underestimated the Harappans and their chief, and that his people's Vedic knowledge was not enough to guarantee success. He vowed to return, wiser and humbler, and to approach the Harappans with a newfound respect and understanding.

As Purusha departed, Baguhara couldn't shake off the memories of past conflicts and tensions between their peoples. The Aryans had always been a thorn in their side, their aggressive expansion and disregard for Harappan boundaries, a constant source of friction. "How can I trust them now?" Baguhara thought.

With a sense of resolve, Baguhara knew he had acted with conviction. "I will protect our people and our future, no matter the cost."

As the fate of Harappa and the future of the Indus Valley region hung in the balance, the Harappans and Aryans began to clash over language, culture, and power. The outcome was unknown, as they struggled to find a path forward amidst the complexities of their vastly different cultures.

Chapter Two

A Night at the Harappan Tavern

The next day, Purusha, accompanied by his fellow Aryan warriors, Ashwin and Varuna, ventured into the heart of Harappa's bustling marketplace. Their mission was to mingle with the locals, gather information, and spread the influence of their Vedic culture.

The aroma of exotic spices - cardamom, cinnamon, and saffron wafted through the air, enticing their senses. The clanging of copper pots filled the atmosphere, creating a vibrant symphony that echoed off the mud-brick buildings. The warm sun beat down upon their skin, its golden rays illuminating the vibrant colors of the market stalls - crimson, emerald, and sapphire.

As they navigated the crowded streets, the Aryans marveled at the exotic sights and sounds of the Harappan city. Ashwin, an astute warrior with a hint of superiority over Purusha, leaned into whisper, "Remember, Purusha, we must be strategic in our approach. These Harappans are not to be underestimated." His voice was laced with a subtle disdain, born from his belief in the Aryans' cultural and intellectual superiority. Yet, beneath his confident exterior, Ashwin struggled with high expectations from his parents. As the eldest son of a respected Aryan family, he felt the burden of responsibility and wanted to prove himself worthy of his father's name.

Purusha agreed, with his gaze moving across the crowd. "I understand, Ashwin. However, I cannot resist feeling a sense of amazement towards the grandeur of this city. It's different from anything we have seen before."

Ashwin smiled. "That's because you're too busy admiring the architecture, Purusha. Keep your focus on the task at hand. We need to identify potential allies and gather information on their political landscape."

Purusha nodded, his expression serious. "You're right, as always, Ashwin. Let's get to work."

They eventually stumbled upon a lively tavern, where merchants and traders gathered to share stories and enjoy local delicacies.

Purusha's warm smile and genuine interest in the traders' stories quickly won them over, and soon he was laughing with the group. They welcomed him with open arms, offering cups of sweet, fermented beverages and plates of spicy, fragrant dishes.

His chiseled features and piercing gaze captivated the attention of the traders, who couldn't help but be drawn to his effortless charm. His broad shoulders and athletic build, honed from years of martial training, commanded respect, while his quick wit and easy humor put even the most skeptical strangers at ease. Yet, beneath his confident exterior, Purusha harbored a deep empathy for others, a compassion that drove him to seek understanding and connection with those around him.

Ashwin, however, struggled to connect with the locals. His rigid adherence to Aryan customs and his disdain for the Harappans' "unclean" practices made him come across as aloof and superior. Harappan's indulgence in fermented beverages and rich, spicy cuisine, their acceptance of more relaxed social norms, were anathema to Ashwin. He saw them as a sign of weakness and chaos, and believed that the Aryans' stricter, more disciplined way of life was the only path to true greatness.

Varuna, on the other hand, was taken away by the Harappans' advanced irrigation systems and engaged in a conversation with a local engineer. His curious mind was always trying to learn and understand the intricacies of the world around him. With a thirst for knowledge and a passion for humanity, Varuna saw the world as a complex puzzle waiting to be deciphered. His eyes became bright as he listened to the engineer's explanations, his mind churning with ideas and questions.

The local engineer, a grizzled old man with a kind face, gestured animatedly as he explained the intricacies of the system. "You know, Varuna, our ancestors built this system to withstand the mighty Indus River's floods. We use a combination of canals, dams, and reservoirs to store and distribute water to our crops."

Varuna nodded eagerly. "I see. And what about the materials you use for the canals? They seem incredibly durable."

The engineer chuckled. "Ah, that's the secret to our success. We use a combination of clay, brick, and stone to construct the canals. It's a technique that's been passed down through generations of Harappan engineers."

The night wore on, and Purusha became lost in the tales of Harappan heroes and legends, his imagination sparked by the stories of the people who had built a civilization so grand and yet so different from their own. He began to see beyond the cultural differences and recognized the shared humanity that connected them all.

Just as the night was reaching its peak, a group of Harappan soldiers appeared, their armor glinting in the firelight, their eyes fixed disapprovingly on the Aryan strangers. The leader, a stern-faced warrior named Dabira, confronted Purusha and his companions.

"You Aryans may think you're more sophisticated with your language and customs," Dabira sneered, "but you're nothing but barbarians in our eyes. There is no place for communal politics with your unjustified superiority in our society. You must leave our city and our people alone, before things escalate further."

Purusha, sensing the tension, stood up to address the Harappan leader. "We mean no disrespect, Dabira. We come in peace, seeking to learn from each other and forge a new path forward."

Dabira snorted, his expression unyielding. "The only path forward is for you to leave our city, before we show you the true meaning of Harappan hospitality."

Purusha's companions, Ashwin and Varuna, exchanged a nervous glance. They knew that Dabira's words were laced with a veiled threat, and that their presence was tenuous at best.

Purusha's expression remained calm and respectful. "I understand your skepticism, Dabira. But we're not here to conquer or destroy. We're seeking a new way, one that honors the diversity of our cultures and traditions. Can we not find common ground and work towards a brighter future together?"

Dabira's gaze narrowed, his voice cold and menacing. "You expect us to believe that you've changed your ways? That you'll suddenly respect our customs and traditions? I think not. You Aryans are known for your deception. We won't be fooled again."

Purusha's eyes locked onto Dabira's, his voice firm and resolute. "I understand that trust must be earned, Dabira. And I promise you, we will do everything in our power to prove our good intentions. But I ask you, is it not worth a chance to forge a new path, one that benefits both our peoples?"

Dabira's expression softened slightly, his voice taking on a hint of resignation. "I fear it is too late for that, Purusha. Our people have been hurt by outsiders before. We cannot trust so easily again. But I will give you this: leave peacefully, and we will not harm you. That is the most I can offer."

As Dabira spoke, a flicker of memory crossed his mind – one of his uncles had been killed in a raid by a neighboring tribe when he was just a boy. The pain and anger he had felt then still lingered, and he had dedicated his life to protecting his people from outsiders. But as he looked at Purusha, he saw something unexpected, a genuine desire to understand and connect with the Harappans. It was a glimmer of hope that Dabira hadn't seen in a long time, and it gave him a pause.

And with that, the night's camaraderie was shattered, leaving the Aryans to wonder if their mission had just taken a grave turn.

Chapter Three

The Shadow of Envy

As the days passed, Purusha and his companions, Ashwin and Varuna continued to explore Harappa, marveling at the city's advanced architecture, sophisticated irrigation systems, and vibrant marketplaces. The towering granaries, meticulously crafted seals, and intricately designed jewelry left them in awe. The city's planners had carefully designed the streets to maximize ventilation and natural light, creating a sense of airy openness that belied the dense population. The sophisticated drainage system, with its cleverly engineered clay pipes, kept the city clean and hygienic, a marvel of ancient urban planning.

Everywhere they looked, they saw evidence of a refined and cultured people. The intricate mosaics that adorned the walls of the public buildings told stories of myth and legend, while the beautifully crafted pottery and ceramics spoke of a deep understanding of form and function. The city's artisans were masters of their craft, creating exquisite works of art that rivaled anything Purusha had seen in his travels.

The marketplaces were a riot of color and sound, with merchants hawking their wares in a dozen different cadences. The air was thick with the smells of spices, fresh bread, and roasting meats, making their mouths water and their stomachs growl. They marveled at the variety of goods on offer, from fine silks and cottons to glittering gemstones and precious metals.

But it was not just the physical city that impressed them – it was the people themselves. The Harappans were a friendly and welcoming folk, eager to share their knowledge and traditions with these curious strangers. They were a people of great learning and wisdom, with a deep understanding of nature and the mysteries of the world.

As the trio of adventurers delved deeper into the city, they began to realize that Harappa was more than just a collection of buildings and people – it was a living, breathing entity, a vibrant and pulsing heart that beat with a rhythm all its own. And they knew that they would never forget this experience, this glimpse into a world so different from their own.

But alongside their wonder and admiration, they couldn't help but feel a growing sense of envy. Why did this city have such advanced systems and structures, while their own people still lived in nomadic tribes, struggling to survive? Why did the Harappans have access to such wealth and knowledge, while they were left to scrounge and scrape by? The feeling gnawed at them, fueling a desire to learn more, to understand the secrets of this ancient civilization, and perhaps, to claim a piece of its glory for themselves.

"Why do the Harappans get to enjoy such prosperity and wealth, while we Aryans struggle to survive in the harsh steppes?" Ashwin muttered; his voice laced with bitterness.

Purusha frowned in agreement. "It's unfair that they get to hoard all the knowledge of agriculture and irrigation, while we're left in the dark."

Varuna, an intelligent scholar and sage who had studied the Vedas extensively, spoke up. "We should focus on learning from them, rather than coveting their success. We can adapt their innovations to our own needs and improve our own lives. Besides, envy and resentment only lead to suffering. Let's use our knowledge of the Vedas to cultivate a mindset of gratitude and abundance."

But Ashwin's envy had already taken root. "We don't need to learn from them. We just need to take what's rightfully ours. We speak the language of the Gods and Gods have chosen us to be the rulers of this land, not the Harappans."

Purusha's eyes narrowed, his mind racing with the possibilities. "Perhaps Ashwin is right. Maybe it's time we assert our dominance and claim the riches of this city for ourselves without any bloodshed. We must lure Harappans in our way".

Varuna's face fell, disappointment etched on his features. "Ashwin, I'm disappointed in you. You're influencing Purusha with your envy and ambition. Can't you see that this path leads only to destruction?"

Ashwin sneered. "You're just too soft, Varuna. You don't understand the way the world works. Purusha sees the truth now. We don't need your outdated wisdom holding us back."

Ashwin was born into a respected Aryan family, but his childhood was marked by tragedy. His mother died in childbirth, and his father became distant and demanding. Determined to prove himself, Ashwin threw himself into martial training, becoming a skilled warrior and strict adherent to Aryan customs. Despite his tough exterior, he struggled with feelings of inadequacy and failure that carried the weight of his own ambitions.

Varuna's expression turned from disappointment to deepening concern. He had always known Ashwin to be ambitious, but this was different. This was a darkness that threatened to consume them all.

Varuna's family was known for their bravery and martial prowess. From a young age, he trained in the art of warfare, honing his skills with sword and spear. However, unlike his peers, Varuna's true strength lay in his strategic mind and ability to think critically. He devoured ancient texts on warfare and philosophy, seeking to understand the deeper nature of conflict and leadership.

As he grew older, Varuna became disillusioned with the endless wars and skirmishes between rival clans. He began to see the value of diplomacy and cooperation, often advocating for peaceful resolutions to conflicts. His friends saw him as a wise and thoughtful warrior, one who balanced strength with compassion.

"I fear for our future, Ashwin. Your hatred and greed will be our downfall." Varuna said.

"I know what I'm thinking," Ashwin replied, his voice dripping with false confidence, his tone self-assured. "I know what's best for our people." His ignorance was a palpable force, a fog that obscured his judgment and led him down a dangerous path.

As the Aryans continued to simmer in their envy and resentment, the seeds of conflict were sown. The Harappans, oblivious to the growing tensions, continued to welcome the strangers with open arms, unaware of the storm that was brewing on the horizon.

Chapter Four

The Allure of the Aryan

While the Aryans continued to mingle with the Harappans, an unexpected phenomenon emerged. The upper-class Harappan women, known for their dark-skinned beauty and grace, began to take notice of the Aryan men. They were drawn to their rugged charm, their confident stride, and their piercing blue eyes.

Princess Armita, the daughter of Baguhara, found herself especially taken with Purusha's charisma and linguistic skills. She was a vision of loveliness, with skin as smooth as ivory, hair as black as the night sky, and eyes that sparkled like the brightest stars in the sky.

But it was not just her physical beauty that drew people to her - her gentle heart, her kindness, and her compassion towards all living beings were virtues that shone forth from her very being. She would often glance at Purusha during daily outings, her heart fluttering with excitement. His ability to converse in multiple languages, including her own, was a quality she found particularly endearing. Her eyes sparkled as she watched Purusha recite his poems and sing with a voice that was like the soothing melody of the heart's deepest feeling. His words seemed to weave a spell of love and longing, transporting her to a realm of beauty and passion.

One day, as they walked along the city's central canal, Armita finally gathered the courage to approach Purusha.

"Purusha, I must confess, I find your stories and poems enchanting," she said softly.

Purusha, taken aback by the princess's forwardness, stuttered, "T-thank you, Princess. I'm glad you enjoy them."

Armita's eyes sparkled with mischief. "I enjoy more than just your stories, Purusha. I enjoy the way you speak, the way you move, the way you make me feel."

Purusha's face flushed with surprise, but he couldn't deny the attraction he felt towards the princess. "Armita, I...I don't know what to say. You are a princess, and I am just a guest in the city."

Armita's smile faltered for a moment before she regained her composure. "Perhaps, but I am also a woman, and I know what I want. And what I want is to get to know you better, Purusha."

As they wandered through the bustling streets of Harappa, Armita turned to Purusha with a curious gaze. "Tell me, Purusha, what you thought of our culture and people when you first arrived in our city?"

Purusha's eyes sparkled with enthusiasm. "Armita, I was struck by the beauty and sophistication of Harappa. The intricate pottery, the vibrant marketplaces, and the stunning architecture - all of it was so impressive. And the people... I was warmly received by the people of Harappa. I was struck by the kindness, hospitality, and generosity of the Harappans."

Armita's face lit up with pride. "That means a lot to me, Purusha. We take pride in our culture and our city. But I sense there was something more that caught your attention - something that surprised you, perhaps?"

Purusha's expression turned thoughtful. "I must admit, I was surprised by the grandeur of the Great Bath. Its sheer scale and beauty took my breath away. And the city's architecture - the precise brickwork, the elegant doorways, and the towering walls... it's truly a marvel of engineering and design."

Armita's laughter was like music. "Ha! we Harappans are known for our skill and craftsmanship. And I'm glad you noticed. We make our own way and contribute to our society in our own unique ways."

Purusha smiled, his eyes shining with admiration. "I am glad to have seen it for myself, Armita. Your city and your people are truly admirable. And the women... I was surprised by their independence and assertiveness. In my own culture, women often have more limited roles, but here... I saw women merchants, artisans, and even warriors! It was refreshing and inspiring to see."

Armita's smile was captivating. "We, Harappan women are known for our strength and determination. And I'm glad you noticed."

As they walked further, they came across a group of artisans crafting beautiful pottery. Purusha's eyes widened in amazement. "Armita, this pottery is exquisite! The designs, the colors... it's like nothing I've ever seen before."

Armita gave a subtle nod of understanding. "Our artisans are skilled indeed. They spend years perfecting their craft, and their hard work shows in every piece they create."

Purusha's head tilted, his eyes thoughtful. "I see. I can feel the energy of this place, the sense of community and shared purpose. It's truly remarkable. We Aryans want to be part of this great legend through mutual cooperation and cultural exchange."

Armita smiled, her voice filled with warmth. "We are a proud people, and we welcome those who appreciate our culture and our city."

As they continued their stroll, the tension between them was palpable. Armita's laughter was like music, sweet and alluring. "Wisdom is for the wise, Purusha. I am a woman who follows her heart, and my heart tells me that we are meant to be together".

* * *

Purusha knew that he had to make a decision, one that would affect not only his own fate but also the fate of his people. Suddenly, memories from his past flooded his thoughts. He remembered the starry nights spent gazing up at the celestial expanse, wondering about the secrets beyond their tribal lands. He recalled the ancient text etched on a crumbling stone, speaking of a great civilization where wisdom and knowledge flowed like rivers. The words had ignited a fire within him, driving him to leave his parents in search of this fabled land.

Purusha's thoughts raced back to his parents, who had encouraged his curiosity despite their reservations. He remembered his father's wise words: "A leader must be willing to venture into the unknown, to seek knowledge and wisdom." His mother's stories of their ancestors' bravery and the gods' favor also echoed in his mind.

Meanwhile, Ashwin saw the potential for political gain. "Purusha, you have a great opportunity to win over the heart of the Harappan Princess. Use this to the advantage of our Aryans. Marry Princess Armita and secure an alliance with the royal family." His voice was laced with a hunger for power, a desire to prove himself as a master strategist. Ashwin's ambition had always driven him to manipulate others, to use their strengths for his own gain. And now, he saw Purusha's relationship with Armita as the perfect opportunity to further his own interests.

Purusha wandered back and forth, his mind racing with thoughts of Armita. Her words echoed in his mind: "Wisdom is for the wise, Purusha. I am a woman who follows her heart, and my heart tells me that we are meant to be together."

He couldn't deny the attraction he felt towards her - her intelligence, her wit, and her beauty had captivated him from the start. But it was more than that. He admired her strength, her compassion, and her passion for her people.

In that moment, Purusha realized that his journey had brought him full circle. He was faced with a choice that would determine the course of his life and the fate of his people. The allure of the Harappan princess and the promise of power tempted him, but he knew that his decision must align with the values of his ancestors and the gods he revered.

Varuna, ever the voice of reason, cautioned against such a move. "We must be careful not to offend the Harappans. We are guests in this city, and we should not abuse their hospitality." Varuna's calm demeanor was a stark contrast to Ashwin's fervor, and he often found himself tempering his friend's impulsive nature.

Ashwin snorted. "Hospitality? Ha! The Harappans are weak, Varuna. They think only of trade and commerce. We must seize this opportunity to strengthen our position."

Varuna's voice remained calm, but firm. "I disagree, Ashwin. We must respect the Harappans' customs and traditions. We cannot simply take advantage of their kindness."

Ashwin's face twisted in frustration. "You always err on the side of caution, Varuna. Sometimes I think you forget that we are Aryans, destined for greatness."

Varuna's eyes narrowed. "I have not forgotten, Ashwin. But greatness comes not from exploiting others, but from building strong relationships and alliances."

As Purusha pondered his decision, Ashwin's words echoed in his mind like a tantalizing whisper. The promise of power, the thrill of adventure, and the allure of the Harappan Princess all beckoned him to take a chance. He thought of his parents' stories, of the great leaders who had expanded their tribe's territories and secured their people's future. He thought of his own destiny; of the mark he wanted to leave on the world.

But Varuna's cautionary voice lingered, a gentle breeze that tempered the flames of ambition. Purusha knew that his friend spoke from a place of wisdom, that the consequences of his actions would ripple far beyond his own desires.

"What will you do, Purusha?" Varuna asked, his eyes filled with concern. "Will you follow your heart or your duty?"

Chapter Five

The Harappan Resistance

As Purusha's relationship with Princess Armita deepened, the Harappan priests and nobles grew increasingly uneasy. They saw the Aryans as a threat to their way of life, and Purusha's influence over the princess as a dangerous betrayal.

Dabira, the chief advisor to Baguhara, entered the throne room with his face full of concern. "Baguhara, our chief, I bring news that troubles me," he said, his voice laced with worry.

Baguhara looked up from his throne, his face stern but curious. "Speak, Dabira. What's amiss?"

"Purusha, the Aryan leader, has been spending time with our princess, Armita," Dabira replied, his voice gentle but urgent. "I fear his influence may be swaying her from our ways, and I worry for her future and the future of our people."

Baguhara's expression softened, his brow furrowed in concern. "I understand your worries, Dabira. But let us not jump to conclusions. Perhaps Armita sees good in the Aryans, and we should hear from her."

"We must be cautious, your Majesty," Dabira urged. "The Aryans are a powerful force, and we must protect our way of life." Dabira's voice was firm but respectful.

"The cost of inaction will be far greater, your Majesty. I am worried about our future generations. If we do not defend ourselves, we will lose everything that makes us who we are. Our culture, our traditions, our very identity will be erased. Is that truly a price we are willing to pay?"

Baguhara nodded thoughtfully. "I agree, Dabira. Compromising ourselves won't be an option. Let me talk to Armita, but meanwhile, gather our warriors and prepare for the likelihood of a conflict."

As Dabira departed to rally his warriors, Baguhara's thoughts turned to his daughter. He hoped she would come to understand the necessity of his actions and not let her feelings for Purusha cloud her judgment. His heart filled with concern, fearing that her innocence and compassion might be exploited by the Aryans. He wished she could see the world with the same clarity as he did but knew that her youth and idealism made that impossible. Still, he hoped that in time, she would come to see the wisdom in his approach and not be swayed by the Aryans' charms.

Meanwhile, Armita's heart was torn apart by the conflicting demands of her loyalty and her love for Purusha. Her duty to her people pulled her one way, while her soul's longing pulled her in another direction. A whirlpool of emotions raged within her, leaving her lost and alone.

She tried to reason with her father, but he was resolute in his opposition to the Aryans.

"Father, please listen to me," Armita implored, her voice filled with desperation. "Purusha and his people do not pose any problem. They come in peace, seeking to learn from us and trade with us."

Baguhara's expression remained skeptical. "I've heard his words, Armita. But actions speak louder than words. What has he done to prove his intentions?"

Armita hesitated, searching for the right words. "It's not just what he's done, Father. It's how he makes me feel. He listens; he cares...he sees me in a way no one else does."

Baguhara's gaze softened, but his voice remained firm. "I understand how you feel, Armita, but I cannot ignore the risks. The Aryans' influence threatens our traditions, our way of life, and our economic stability. If I don't act, their ideas could erode the foundations of our kingdom, leaving our people vulnerable. I will not stand idly while our heritage is destroyed."

* * *

A few days passed. The Aryan encampment is nestling in the warmth of a sunny afternoon, with tents pitched in the shaded trees on the outskirts of Harappa. Men are lounging, their faces carefree and their laughter carrying on the breeze. Children are playing and laughing. Women are finishing up daily chores while keeping an eye on their children. The elderly with limited mobility are sitting and watching over the valley.

Purusha is spending time with his closest friends, Ashwin and Varuna, sharing stories and enjoying each other's company, with a sense of brotherhood and shared purpose.

Just at that moment, Harappans launched a surprise attack on the Aryan encampment. The Harappan warriors, hidden behind the nearby trees, emerged with a fierce battle cry. The sun was high overhead, casting a golden glow over the bloody battlefield.

The Aryans, caught off guard, scrambled to respond. Purusha, his sword flashing in the sunlight, rallied his comrades, shouting orders to form a defensive line. Ashwin and Varuna fought valiantly alongside him, their swords clashing with the Harappan warriors.

But the Harappans had the advantage of numbers and surprise. They poured in from all sides, their swords and shields a blur of motion. The Aryans fought bravely, but they were vastly outnumbered.

The clash of sword on sword echoed through the valley. The thud of shields colliding, and the cries of the wounded filling the air. Purusha, his sword flashing in the sunlight, fought with a ferocity that inspired his comrades. But the Harappans were relentless, their numbers seemingly endless.

Ashwin was overwhelmed by the power of Harappans. He stumbled backward, his sword slipping from his grasp. Varuna rushed to his side, fighting off the Harappan warriors, but they were too strong. Ashwin fell; his dreams of conquest shattered.

Varuna was gravely injured, his fate uncertain. Purusha, surrounded by the Harappan warriors, faced Dabira's wrathful gaze.

Purusha, his sword trembling with exhaustion, looked up at Dabira with fierce determination. "We came in peace," he said, his voice firm. "We sought only to learn from you and trade with you. Why have you turned against us?"

Dabira's expression twisted in anger. "You have corrupted our princess, Purusha. You have turned her against her own people. You will pay for your treachery."

With a swift stroke of his sword, Dabira ended Purusha's life, sending a message to the Aryans: leave Harappa, or face the consequences.

The Harappans had fought back, determined to protect their culture and their city. But at what cost? With a heavy toll on the Aryan side, the conflict had left deep scars, and the future of the region dangling in uncertainty.

* * *

Princess Armita's heart felt like it had been shattered into a million pieces when she heard the news of Purusha's death. She had tried to convince her father to see the good in Purusha. But her words had fallen on deaf ears. Now, she was left to face the devastating consequences of her father's actions.

Armita felt a numbness wash over her, as if her emotions had been drained from her body. She couldn't think of living in a world without Purusha, without his warm smile and his gentle gesture. She felt like she was thrown into a sea of grief, unable to find a lifeline to cling to.

As she walked through the city streets, she saw familiar people. But everything felt different now. The market stalls, once filled with lively chatter, looked lifeless now. The streets, once bustling with activity, seemed like an endless desert. She felt like she was walking through a dense forest and no one around. She longed to see Purusha's face again, to hear his voice, to feel his presence beside her. But it was all gone, lost forever in the chaos of conflict with Aryans.

As Baguhara reflected on his actions, he couldn't shake off the feeling of resentment towards the Aryans. "Why did they have to come here?" he thought to himself. "Why did they have to disrupt our way of life?" He remembered the countless warnings from Dabira and the other priests, warning him of the dangers of Aryan influence. "I was right to protect our people," he justified. "I was right to defend our traditions."

But as he looked at his daughter, Armita, he saw the depth of her sorrow. He saw the pain in her eyes, the pain he had caused. "What have I done?" he thought, his resentment slowly giving way to regret. "What have I done to my own daughter?" He realized that his actions, though motivated by a desire to protect his people, had caused harm to those he loved.

He remembered the time Armita had come to him, pleading with him to see the good in Purusha and his people. He had dismissed her, thinking he knew what was best for their people. He had let his fear of the unknown and his pride in Harappan heritage cloud his judgment.

Baguhara's emotional struggle intensified as he grappled with the consequences of his actions. He felt the weight of his daughter's grief, the burden of his own regret, and the pressure of his people's expectations. He wondered if he had made a terrible mistake, if he had let his fear and pride guide him instead of wisdom and compassion.

"Why did I not listen to Armita?" he thought, his mind racing with doubts. "Why did I not consider the possibility of peace?" He felt a deep sense of sorrow, knowing that his actions had led to the loss of innocent lives and the suffering of his own daughter. "I caused pain for my own daughter. She will never forgive me." The weight of his daughter's sorrow threatened to consume him

As Baguhara navigated the complexities of his emotions, he began to see a glimmer of hope. He realized that he had the power to make amends, to find a path towards healing and reconciliation. He knew that it wouldn't be easy, that it would require courage and humility. But he was willing to try, for the sake of his daughter, his people, and the future of their city.

* * *

A few days passed. Baguhara's expression was somber as he looked at his daughter. His eyes met Armita's, and he saw the depths of her sorrow. She looked with eyes that revealed a soul suffering from sadness, her red and swollen eyes showing the tears she cried quietly.

"Father," she murmured, "I miss him so much. Purusha was my everything."

"My child, I understand that my actions have brought you grief. I was trying to protect our culture and our city, but I see now that my actions were misguided."

Armita replied, her voice firm but measured, "You were not just misguided, Father. You were wrong. You let your fear and pride guide you, and you ignored the voices of those who tried to reason with you."

Baguhara tilted his head thoughtfully. "I understand that my mistakes have caused suffering, and for that, I am truly sorry. But I hope you can also see that I was trying to do what I thought was best for our people."

Armita's expression softened slightly. "I understand that, Father. But the cost has been too high. We must find a way to move forward, to heal the wounds we have inflicted on each other."

Baguhara bent forward, his eyes filled with a mix of regret and determination. "I agree, my child. And I am willing to listen, to find a path towards healing and reconciliation."

Armita's heart felt heavy, weighed down by the grief that had consumed her. She knew that her father's words were genuine, and she couldn't help but wonder if it was too late. Had they gone too far? Had they caused too much harm?

Armita felt a sense of emptiness, a feeling that she was going through a void, devoid of hope and purpose. She longed to see Purusha's smile again, to hear his laughter, to feel his warmth.

As she walked away from her father, she remembered her mother, who had passed away when she was twelve years old. Her mother had always been a source of comfort and strength, and Armita wished she was there now to offer guidance and support. She closed her eyes and whispered a silent prayer, hoping that her mother was watching over her from heaven.

"Mother, I need your guidance now more than ever," she whispered. "Purusha is gone, and I am left to pick up the pieces. Please help me find the strength to move forward, to find a way to heal the wounds of this conflict."

But little did Armita know that her father's actions would have far-reaching consequences that would ultimately change the lives of Harappans with unprecedented outcomes.

Chapter Six

The Aryan Cultural Expansion

As the days passed slowly, Armita felt the weight of her grief over the loss of Purusha. She had loved him with all her heart, and his death had left her feeling lost and alone.

The memories of their time together now felt bittersweet, a reminder of what she had lost.

Varuna, too, was consumed by sorrow. He had considered Purusha a brother, and the pain of his absence was a constant reminder of the fragility of life and the devastating consequences of conflict.

He remembered the countless battles they had fought side by side, the shared stories of their ancestors, and the laughter they had exchanged around campfires.

One day, Varuna attempted to console Armita over the loss of her beloved Purusha, despite his own grief and pain.

As they sat together in the quiet courtyard, they spoke in hushed tones, their voices gentle and respectful, as they delved into the intricacies of their cultures...

"I'm proud of my Harappan heritage," Armita said, her voice soft and gentle. "The advanced irrigation, the intricate architecture... it's a tribute to our ancestors' ingenuity. But it's not just the physical structures that make our culture so rich. It's the stories, the legends, the myths that have been passed down through generations, carrying the wisdom and values of our people."

"Your cities are indeed impressive," Varuna replied, his voice filled with admiration. "But our Aryan culture has its own unique strengths. Our understanding of astronomy, mathematics, and philosophy has allowed us to make great strides in knowledge and wisdom. And our epics, like the Rigveda, contain timeless wisdom and spiritual guidance, revealing the human condition."

"I see beauty in that," Armita said, her voice soft and contemplative. "But sometimes, I feel too attracted to what Aryans have to offer and I worry that your culture may overshadow our own, erasing the unique traditions and customs that make us who we are. Our artisans, our craftsmen, our traders... they all have stories to tell, skills to share, and experiences that have shaped our culture in ways that are just as valuable as your own."

"I understand your concern," Varuna said, his voice filled with empathy. "But I believe our cultures can complement each other, like the threads of a tapestry, weaving together to create a richer, more vibrant whole."

Armita's face lit up with a thoughtful expression. "I like that image. And I think you're right. We can learn so much from each other and grow together in ways that we never thought possible. But it's not just about sharing knowledge or traditions. It's about understanding the heart of each other's culture – the values, the beliefs, the dreams, the fears... that's what makes us who we are, and that's what will make our friendship truly meaningful."

Varuna smiled, his eyes sparkling with insight. "Exactly! We're not just talking about our cultures, we're talking about our souls – the deepest, most intimate parts of ourselves. And when we share our souls, that's when the real magic happens – the magic of connection, of understanding, and of unity."

* * *

While Varuna and Armita were discussing the uniqueness of their cultures, some Aryan priests, undeterred by the loss of their warriors, devised a new strategy to win over the Harappans. They began to introduce their complex culture, showcasing their knowledge of astronomy and philosophy.

Vivid tales of the Vedic gods and goddesses, with their intricate mythologies, captivated the Harappan imagination. The Aryans' poetic traditions, rich in metaphor and allegory, resonated deeply with the Harappan love of storytelling.

With the advice from Armita, Varuna took on a new role as a cultural ambassador. He shared the Aryan art of yoga, teaching the Harappans the secrets of breath control and meditation.

"May our breath be as one, our minds as clear as the Indus," Varuna said, as he guided the Harappans through their first yoga practice.

Meanwhile, the Aryan women, with their fair skin and silky hair, fascinated the Harappan men. They introduced the Harappans to their traditional dances, poetry, and their intricate music, played on the veena and flute.

"This music speaks to my soul," said a Harappan warrior, mesmerized by the haunting melodies.

The Harappans, enchanted by these new cultural offerings, began to see the Aryans in a different light.

They started to adopt Aryans' music and poetry, blending them with their own traditional ways.

Baguhara, impressed by the Aryan wisdom and artistry, extended the peace gesture. He invited the Aryan leaders to a grand cultural festival, where both communities could share their heritage and forge a new bond.

"Let us celebrate our differences, and find common ground in our shared humanity," Baguhara declared, as he welcomed the Aryan leaders to the festival.

The festival, held on the sun-kissed banks of the Indus, was a kaleidoscope of colors and rhythms. Aryan musicians played the veena and flute, their melodies intertwining with the Harappan drumbeats and the sweet harmonies of the Aryan women's chanting.

The air was thick with the fragrance of sandalwood and jasmine, and the sky was ablaze with vibrant kites and lanterns in shades of crimson, emerald, and amber.

The crowd was a sea of smiling faces, full of excitement, as they enjoyed the flavors of spiced delicacies and sweet dishes. Laughter and music filled the air, mixed by the clapping hands. Amidst this joyful celebration, artisans showcased their artwork:

glittering gemstones, delicate pottery, and richly woven textiles that told stories of ancient myths and legends.

As the crowd swayed to the music, a Harappan trader approached an Aryan musician.

"Your music is enchanting!" the trader said. "What inspires your compositions?"

"The rhythms of nature, the songs of our ancestors," replied the musician, his fingers deftly plucking the veena strings. "We seek to harmonize with the universe."

"Fascinating!" said the trader. "In Harappa, we too have a deep connection with nature, but our music is more percussive, driven by the beat of drums."

"Ah, I've noticed," said the musician. "Your drumbeats are infectious! Perhaps we can blend our styles, create something new and beautiful."

As they spoke, a group of Aryan dancers took to the stage, their intricate footwork and graceful movements mesmerizing the crowd.

"Your dance is like a prayer, a devotion to the divine," said a Harappan artisan, his eyes filled with admiration.

"Indeed, we seek to honor the gods through our movements," replied the Aryan dancer, her hands gesturing gracefully. "But tell me, what inspires your artistry?"

"The stories of our ancestors, the myths of our land," said the artisan. "We seek to capture the essence of our culture in every pottery, every carving."

"Beautiful!" said the dancer. "We too have our epics, our stories of heroes and gods. Perhaps we can share our tales, inspire each other's art."

As the sun began to set, the sky transformed into a canvas of pink and orange hues, and the festival reached its climax with a grand finale of drumrolls, leaving the audience in a state of enchantment and awe.

"Varuna, I feel a sense of belonging I've never known before," Armita said, a smile spreading across her face.

"The festival has shown us that our cultures are not separate threads, but intertwined fibers," Varuna replied, his voice filled with enthusiasm. "We're breaking down barriers, Armita!"

"In every dance, every song, every shared story, I see a future where our people are united," Armita said, her eyes filled with excitement.

Varuna nodded vigorously. "A future where our differences are celebrated, and our similarities bring us together!"

"This is the beginning of a new era," said an Aryan poet, as he recited a poem in Sanskrit in praise of the Harappan kingdom:

Sindhu sangame mahanagaram

(In the confluence of the Indus, a great city)

Harappa janah susamskrtah

(The people of Harappa are well-cultured)

Tesam nagaram suvibhaktam

(Their city is well-planned)

Rajna tesam priyatamena sasitam

(By their king, who is dear to them, it is ruled)

Vijnanam tesam suvistrtam

(Their knowledge is very extensive)

Samskrtih tesam suvirajita

(Their culture is very radiant)

Tesam lipih ratnam sudiptam

(Their script is a brilliant gem)

Rajnah tesam hrdi sudrdham

(It is firmly established in the king's heart)

Vayamaryah tesam darsanena praptah

(We Aryans have obtained their vision)

Tesam prajah antarnirjvalanti

(Their people are shining inwardly)

Rajnah tesam dharmapalako hasto

(The king's hand is the protector of their law)

Prajah tesam sumukhi sampada prapta

(Their people have obtained great prosperity)

The last drumroll faded away and the festival ended with a resounding clapping of hands echoing across the grounds. The crowd dispersed, carrying with them memories of the vibrant performances, the delicious food, and the warmth of newfound friendships.

As Armita departed, her mind wandered to Purusha. "This festival is like a tribute to him," she thought, "a celebration of the connection we shared.". Tears pricked at the corners of her eyes as she tried to smile, lost in the bittersweet memory of their time together.

* * *

But, amidst this cultural renaissance, a new challenge emerged. A group of Harappan fundamentalists, opposed to the Aryan influence, began to secretly plot against the Chief and Aryans.

"We cannot let our traditions be erased by these foreigners," said a fundamentalist, his voice filled with passion. "We must protect our way of life, no matter the cost."

"But what about the progress we've made?" argued another. "The Aryans have brought new ideas, a new way of life...we've learned so much from them."

"Progress?" sneered the first. "You call it progress to forget our own gods, our own customs? To become like them, weak and divided? No, we must resist, before it's too late."

"We must act, and fast. We can't let them destroy everything we've built," said the first.

"But what can we do? They are playing nicely, waiting for their moment to strike," replied the second.

"We need to find a way to teach them, to make them understand that we mean no harm," suggested the second.

"Understanding? They don't want to understand. They want to destroy," said the first.

"Then we must find a way to stop them, before it's too late," said the second.

"But how?"

"We will find a way. We always do. We are the sons of the Indus, and we will not be defeated so easily," said the second.

"We must be careful, though. We can't let our guard down. They are clever, and they will strike when we least expect it," warned the first.

"You're right. We need to be vigilant. We need to protect our people, our culture, at all costs," agreed the second.

The conversation continued, the two fundamentalists discussing their plans, their voices hushed but determined, their minds churning with strategies and desired outcomes.

This development threatened to undermine the fragile peace and cultural exchange between the Harappans and Aryans, imperiling the delicate bond they had forged. The very fabric of their relationship, woven with such hope and promise, now seems to be unraveling, thread by thread, leaving the future of their alliance hanging precariously in the balance.

Will Chief Baguhara and the Aryan leaders be able to navigate this new challenge and maintain the harmony between their people? Or will the whispers of dissent and hatred tear them asunder? Only time will tell if the bonds of friendship and mutual respect can withstand the forces of intolerance and fear.

Chapter Seven

The Rise of Fundamentalism

As the days passed, a dark shadow crept across the valley, threatening to extinguish the flame of peace. Chamba, the enigmatic leader of the Harappan fundamentalists, secretly sowed seeds of doubt and mistrust among his people. His followers, like misguided souls, spread lies and half-truths about the Aryans, their words fueled by Chamba's charisma and persuasive power.

Chamba's own family had been affected by the cultural exchange between the two civilizations. His sister, who had married an Aryan man, had abandoned the traditional Harappan ways and embraced the Aryan customs. Chamba saw this as a betrayal, and it fueled his determination to protect the Harappan culture and traditions from what he saw as the corrupting influence of the Aryans.

But Chamba's hatred for the Aryans went deeper. His father, a respected Harappan priest, had been killed in a skirmish with Aryan warriors many years ago. Chamba's mother, consumed by grief and anger, had raised him on stories of Aryan brutality and Harappan superiority. Chamba's heart burned with a desire for revenge, and he saw the cultural exchange as a threat to the very fabric of Harappan society.

As he grew older, Chamba's anger and hatred only intensified. He saw the Aryans as a constant threat, a reminder of the trauma and suffering that his people had endured. He believed that the only way to protect the Harappans was to drive the Aryans out, to reclaim their territory and their culture, and to restore the Harappan way of life.

Chamba's followers saw him as a hero, a champion of the Harappan people. They believed that he was the only one who truly understood the threat that the Aryans posed, and that he was the only one who could save them.

But Chamba's obsession with the Aryans had consumed him. He saw everything through the lens of his hatred, and he was willing to do whatever it took to achieve his goal of a Harappan-only society. He was a complex and nuanced character, driven by a toxic mix of pain, anger, and ideology.

The whispers of Chamba's followers grew louder, echoing through the temples and villages. "Don't trust them, they'll cheat you blind. They detest our beloved Mother Goddess and seek to erase our traditions and impose their own customs upon us."

The people's voices grew louder, their fists clenched in anger. Chamba shouted, "Rise up, Harappans! Defend your way of life! Defend your Mother Goddess!" The air was thick with tension, the atmosphere heavy with uncertainty.

* * *

Varuna, being wise, sensed the growing danger and sought out the Harappan chief, Baguhara, to warn him of the impending storm. He found the chief pacing in his chambers, his brow furrowed in concern, his eyes darting towards the windows as if he didn't know how to respond to the growing influence of fundamentalists.

"Your Majesty, the fundamentalists are a threat not just to the Aryans, but to the very fabric of our newfound peace," Varuna urged, his voice low and urgent.

Baguhara's expression turned grave, his voice laced with worry. "Varuna, I fear you speak the truth. I have been trying to negotiate with Chamba, but he seems to be driven by a fanatic's zeal. I do not want another bloodshed by our own people. I fear we are running out of time."

* * *

But before Baguhara could respond, Chamba, with his followers, ambushed the unsuspecting Aryans while they were leaving Harappa. The Aryans, still reeling from a previous attack, were feared to be facing another brutal onslaught. Varuna found himself in the middle of the fight. The battle scene was chaotic, with swords clashing and unarmed Aryans crying for help.

Varuna fought vigorously, his sword slicing through fundamentalists with deadly accuracy. But he was outnumbered by Chamba followers, and soon he was surrounded by them.

Just as everything seemed lost, a group of Harappan warriors, led by Baguhara's military leader, Rishasad, arrived on the scene. As he charged into battle, his sword and spear moving in perfect synchrony, Rishasad's mind was focused on one thing: defeating the fundamentalists and restoring peace to his kingdom.

Rishasad's men followed him without hesitation. His tactical expertise and bravery inspired his troops, fought with intensity that matched their determination, their shouts creating tension among the Chamba followers.

The fight continued, with the two groups colliding in a chaotic mix of weapons and wounded people. Varuna stumbled; his vision blurred by pouring blood. But Rishasad was there to support him, their swords moving in perfect synchrony as they fought off the enemy. The air was filled with the thunder of swords and cries of the wounded echoing through the valley, as the two sides engaged in a violent frenzy.

Chamba, his eyes blazing with hatred, singled out Varuna. "You'll destroy our culture, our Mother Goddess!" Chamba snarled.

"We mean no harm, Chamba," Varuna replied. "We seek peace and understanding."

"Lies!" Chamba screamed, striking at Varuna with renewed ferocity, his sword raised for the killing blow. But Rishasad was quicker, his sword flashing in the sunlight as he struck down Chamba. The enemy lines wavered, their resolve broken, and the Harappans and Aryans pressed their advantage, cutting down the remaining Chamba's followers with merciless precision.

Finally, the battle was over, the only sound was the heavy breathing of the victors and the cries of the wounded. Varuna lay on the ground, his body battered and bruised, but his eyes locked onto Rishasad's, and he nodded slightly, his lips curling into a faint smile as he clasped Rishasad's arm in a gesture of gratitude.

"We Harappans will not let our friendship with Aryans be destroyed by the forces of hate," Rishasad said, his voice firm and resolute. "We stand together, united against those who seek to divide us."

Rishasad's words were not just a statement of solidarity; they resonated with his own dedication to his people and chief Baguhara.

But as they walked away from the battlefield, the shadows seemed to grow longer, the wind whispering ominous warnings of the trials yet to come. The fundamentalists may have been defeated, but the darkness that drove them still lurked, waiting for its next victim.

* * *

As the dust settled, Baguhara turned to Varuna and said, "I am ashamed that my own people have brought shame upon our kingdom. But I promise you, we will not rest until we have rooted out the evil of fundamentalism and restored peace to our kingdom."

Varuna's movements were slow, his body a map of bruises and cuts that ached with every step, tilted forward in appreciation. "Your words are wise, Your Majesty. Let us work together to build a brighter future, where all can live in harmony and respect."

And so, the Aryans and Harappans continued their journey, united in their quest for peace and understanding, but aware that the road ahead would be fraught with danger and uncertainty.

Chapter Eight

The Shadow of Inferiority

As the cultural exchange continued to flourish, a subtle yet insidious notion began to take hold among the Harappans. They started to perceive the Aryans as inherently more intelligent, more refined, and more civilized. This perception slowly crept into their minds, like a whisper in the darkness, sowing seeds of self-doubt and insecurity.

"I don't know how they do it," said one Harappan to another. "Their knowledge of the stars and planets is so vast, it's like they have a direct connection to the gods."

"Yes, and have you heard their poetry?" replied the other. "It's like music to the ears, so beautiful and refined. I feel like our own stories and songs are so crude in comparison."

"I know what you mean," said a third Harappan, joining the conversation. "I've seen their philosophers debating in the marketplace, and it's like they're speaking a language we can't even understand. I feel like we're just simple traders and craftsmen, not worthy of their level of intellect."

Armita felt a growing sense of unease as she watched her people emulate the Aryans. And she wondered, would they ever find their way back to their own true selves?

Baguhara, the chief of Harappans, stood tall, his voice booming through the crowd. "We Harappans have our own distinct strengths and wisdom," he declared. "We have built a civilization that is worthy of pride, with our own innovations, our own art, and our own traditions. We must not compare ourselves to others, but rather celebrate our own achievements."

But despite Baguhara's words, the Harappans' doubts lingered. They began to emulate the Aryans, adopting their customs and attire, hoping to bridge the perceived gap in intelligence and culture. They practiced the Vedic mantras, their voices stumbling over the unfamiliar words.

It was a vulnerability that had been exposed before. The Harappans had faced devastating floods in the past, which had left their cities in ruins and their people displaced. In their desperation, they had turned to the Aryan traditions, seeking solace and protection in the ancient rituals and incantations.

Over time, they had come to believe that the Vedic rituals held the key to their salvation, and that the Aryans, who possessed this knowledge, were therefore superior.

This notion of self-doubt was further fueled after Chamba's attack on Aryans, as the Harappans were filled with a sense of guilt and unease. They had always been a peaceful people, and the violence of the Chamba's attack went against everything they believed in.

As Harappans struggled to keep up with the Aryan pace, they began to lose touch with their own unique identity. Their once-vibrant traditions were gradually replaced by Aryan practices and beliefs. The Harappans' own stories, songs, and poetry were forgotten, replaced by Aryan literature and art. Their philosophers and scholars were no longer valued, as Aryan wisdom was seen as superior.

This belief had been simmering beneath the surface, waiting to be exploited by the Aryans' cultural assimilation.

The Aryans, pleased with this development, encouraged the Harappans to continue down this path.

They offered to share their knowledge and expertise, further solidifying their influence over the region.

As a result, they became even more susceptible to the Aryan culture, embracing their customs and beliefs with a fervor that bordered on desperation. They hoped that by adopting the Vedic mantras and the Aryan way of life, they could protect themselves from future disasters.

As they continued to assimilate, their own distinct culture began to fade. Their once-vibrant traditions, now seen as inferior, were gradually replaced by Aryan practices and beliefs.

And so, the Harappans, in their quest for intellectual and cultural parity, unwittingly surrendered their own individual identity.

Chapter Nine

The Quest for Inner Truth

As the Harappans struggled with cultural appropriation, their men turned inward, seeking solace in philosophy and spirituality. They delved into the mysteries of the human condition, seeking answers to their questions.

"We must look within for truth," said one, his eyes closed in contemplation.

"The external world is an illusion," replied another, his voice filled with conviction.

They developed a deep understanding of human desire, recognizing the fleeting nature of material wealth and power. They sought wisdom within their own hearts and minds.

"The world reflects our minds," said a wise Harappan sage. "We must purify our thoughts to see the truth."

The Harappan men became ascetics, renouncing worldly desires and attachments. They wandered, sharing wisdom and teachings with all who would listen.

"Harappan Rebirth holds the key to understanding," said an ascetic, his eyes filled with compassion.

Their philosophy emphasized unity, interconnectedness, and the cyclical nature of life.

"Life and death are two sides of the same coin," said a Harappan ascetic. "We must embrace both to find peace."

As they deepened their spiritual practices, they experienced deep states of consciousness, revealing hidden truths.

"We're droplets in the ocean of existence," said a Harappan sage. "We must merge with the divine to find wisdom."

But as they delved deeper into their spiritual quest, they began to neglect their responsibilities. Families were slowly dwindling, as the population gently declined. Homes were being abandoned, left to crumble and decay, as the once-thriving civilization was gradually unraveling. The Harappans became increasingly detached from the world around them.

"Husbands and wives are no longer bound by love and duty," lamented a Harappan elder. "Our families are slowly disappearing, and our society is changing in ways we never intended. Our homes, once filled with laughter and life, now stand empty and silent.

The Harappans' obsession with spiritual enlightenment had led them down a path of abandonment and disconnection. Their society was slowly losing its vibrancy, and their people were suffering.

The Aryans, seeing the harm they had caused, knew they had to act, but didn't know where to start. But no one foresaw the magnitude of the transformation that was to come. A transformation that will reshape the destiny of the Harappans, and the future of the Indus Valley.

Chapter Ten

The Weight of Conscience

One evening, Princess Armita and Varuna sat together in the courtyard, their faces etched with concern. They had watched as the Harappans, once a thriving and vibrant civilization, slowly unraveled.

"This is a tragedy, Varuna," Armita said, her voice laced with despair. "The Harappans were once so full of life and laughter. Now, our homes are empty, our families dwindling."

Varuna shook his head, his eyes filled with sorrow. "I know Princess. It's as if they've lost sight of what truly matters. Their pursuit of spiritual enlightenment has consumed them, and they've forgotten the beauty of connection, of community."

Armita's voice cracked with emotion. "I feel so helpless, Varuna. We've tried to reach out to them, to bring them back from the brink of destruction. But they won't listen. They're too far gone."

Varuna's eyes reflected his own despair. "We can't give up, Armita. We must keep trying. We owe it to the Harappans, to their children and their children's children."

As the Harappans continued their spiritual journey, the Aryan priests began to feel a creeping sense of guilt. With Varuna and Armita's relentless efforts, Aryans realized that their actions had caused harm and suffering to the Harappan people, and that their cultural appropriation had erased a vital part of human history.

Their conscience, once silenced by their thirst for power and knowledge, now spoke loudly, urging them to make amends. They saw the error of their ways and understood that their superiority complex had blinded them to the beauty and value of Harappan culture.

The Aryan leaders, filled with remorse, sought out Harappan Chief Baguhara and the Harappan elders. They confessed their wrongdoing, acknowledging the pain they had caused and the cultural heritage they had stolen.

"We have taken away your knowledge, your art, and your customs," they said. "We have erased your legacy and marginalized your people. We come to you now, seeking forgiveness and a chance to make things right."

Baguhara, wise and compassionate, looked upon the Aryans with a mix of sadness and understanding. "We forgive you," he said. "But forgiveness is not enough. You must work to restore what has been lost, to revive our culture and our heritage."

"Justly said, Father," Armita added, her voice firm but gentle. "We Harappans have suffered greatly, but we are willing to put the past behind us and work towards a brighter future, one where our cultures can coexist and flourish."

"We understand, your Majesty," Varuna said, his voice filled with compassion. "We are willing to do the work necessary to make amends. But we need your guidance and trust."

"We trust you, Varuna," Baguhara said, his voice gentle. "But we must see action, not just words. We must see our culture and heritage restored, and our people treated with dignity and respect."

"We will do everything possible to make that happen," the Aryan leader promised. "We will work tirelessly to restore your culture and heritage, and to build a new future based on mutual respect and understanding."

"We must," said Varuna. "And I propose that we establish a great university, where scholars from both communities can come to learn and teach. We must preserve the wisdom of the Harappans and combine it with the knowledge of the Aryans. Together, we can create a new era of enlightenment and progress."

Baguhara nodded in agreement. "Let us build this university, and let it stand as a symbol of hope for our people. Let us work together to create a brighter future, one that honors the diversity and complexity of human culture."

And so, the two communities began a new chapter in their journey, one marked by cooperation, cultural exchange, and a deep appreciation for the diversity of human experience. The Harappans and the Aryans worked together to build the great university, and it became a symbol of their newfound friendship and respect.

Armita felt content with the new development, knowing that her people's culture and heritage would finally be respected and preserved. She walked among the scholars and students at the university, proud to see the Harappan and Aryan youth learning together, their minds and hearts filled with a newfound appreciation for each other's cultures.

And so, the Aryans, humbled and chastened, began the long journey of redemption, working to restore the Harappan culture and heritage, and to build a brighter future for all.

Chapter Eleven

A New Era of Harmony

With the Aryans' apology and commitment to restoration, a new era of harmony began to dawn on the region. The Harappans, seeing the genuine remorse and effort from their former oppressors, began to open their hearts and minds once more.

Together, the two societies started to rebuild and restore the lost cultural heritage of the Harappans. Aryan scholars worked alongside Harappan sages to translate and preserve ancient texts, while Harappan artists collaborated with Aryan craftsmen to recreate lost masterpieces.

One day, as they worked on a new temple, a Harappan artisan turned to an Aryan craftsman and said, "I never thought I'd be working alongside an Aryan, but I'm glad we're doing this together."

The Aryan craftsman replied. "I've learned so much from you already. Our people have much to learn from each other."

Harappan Chief Baguhara and the Aryan leaders worked together to establish a new order, one that celebrated diversity and promoted mutual understanding. They created a council of wise men and women from both societies, tasked with resolving disputes and fostering cooperation. This council became a beacon of hope for the region, a symbol of what could be achieved through forgiveness, respect, and understanding.

Baguhara addressing the council, "Let us make this a priority, my friends. Let us create a new generation of Harappans and Aryans who will grow up together, learning from each other and valuing their diversity. Let us build a future where our children can live in peace and harmony, free from the burdens of our past.

The council members clapped in agreement, and a sense of determination filled the air. They knew that this would not be an easy task, but they were committed to making it a reality.

Princess Armita added, "We must also ensure that our children learn from our mistakes. We must teach them to recognize the signs of hatred and fear, and to stand against them. We must teach them to be brave enough to challenge injustice and to fight for what is right."

Varuna nodded in agreement. "We must also teach them to forgive and to seek understanding. Our people have suffered too long from hatred and fear. It is time for us to heal and to move forward together."

Baguhara said, "I propose that we establish a joint council of Harappan and Aryan leaders, to oversee the education and development of our children. We must work together to create a brighter future for all of us."

The council members applauded, and the meeting ended with a sense of hope and determination. The Harappans and Aryans had finally found a path towards peace and harmony, and they were determined to follow it.

As they left the council chamber, Armita turned to Varuna and said, "I am glad that we are working together towards a common goal. I believe that our children will be the ones to bring about a new era of peace and prosperity."

Varuna smiled. "I share your hope, Princess. Together, we can achieve great things."

As harmony took root, the kingdom prospered. Crops grew tall, rivers flowed clear, and the skies shone bright. The people of the region, once divided, now came together in celebration of their shared humanity.

At a festival celebrating Mother Goddess, Armita said, "We have come a long way from the darkness of our past. Let us continue to walk together towards a brighter future."

As the years passed, the region flourished. Trade and cultural exchange increased, and the Harappans and Aryans became united in their quest for knowledge and progress. The once-lost heritage of the Harappans was revived, and their culture became an integral part of the region's rich tapestry.

The Harappans also shared their expertise in agriculture with the Aryans, teaching them advanced irrigation techniques, crop rotation methods, and how to cultivate crops in challenging terrain. This knowledge helped the Aryans to improve their own agricultural practices, leading to increased food security and prosperity for both communities.

In return, the Aryans shared their knowledge of animal husbandry and metalworking with the Harappans, further enriching the cultural exchange.

And so, the Harappans and Aryans forged a lasting peace, their once-turbulent past now a shining example of the power of forgiveness, cooperation, and the human spirit's capacity for growth and transformation.

Chapter Twelve

A New Era of Unity

As harmony and cooperation between the Harappans and Aryans continued to grow, a new trend emerged: inter-sect marriages became increasingly common. People from both societies began to see beyond their cultural differences, recognizing the beauty of unity and the strength of their combined heritage.

One day, Princess Armita met Bharadwaja, a gentle and wise Aryan priest, with whom she fell deeply in love. Their chance encounter blossomed into a beautiful connection, with long walks along the river, lively debates about philosophy, and quiet moments of understanding.

As they explored each other's worlds, they discovered a shared passion for unity and harmony. Armita was captivated by Bharadwaja's kindness and compassion, while Bharadwaja admired Armita's intelligence and courage. Together, they dreamed of a future where their people could live in peace and prosperity.

* * *

"It is time for our families to come together," said Princess Armita, as she prepared for her wedding to Bharadwaja.

"Our union will be a symbol of hope for a brighter future."

"You are the sunshine that brightens every day," Bharadwaja said, taking her hand in his.

"I'm so grateful to have met you," Armita said, her eyes welling up with tears. "You've opened my eyes to the beauty of your people's wisdom and spirituality. I promise to stand by you, always."

"My love, Armita," Bharadwaja said, his face glowing with joy, "I promise to love and cherish you, now and forever. Together, let's create a brighter future, where our love shines brightly and guides us on our journey."

The wedding ceremony was a vibrant and joyful celebration, with elements of both cultures beautifully intertwined. The ceremony took place in a lush green garden, with intricate flower arrangements and colorful decorations adorning the surroundings.

The pleasant aroma of incense and the soft glow of lanterns filled the air, creating a serene and peaceful ambiance.

Princess Armita looked resplendent in her traditional Harappan attire, with intricate gold jewelry and a delicate veil covering her face. Bharadwaja wore a simple yet elegant Aryan robe, with a sacred thread draped across his shoulder. Together, they walked around the sacred fire, their hands entwined as they recited their vows.

The Harappan drummers beat out a lively rhythm, while the Aryan flautists played a soothing melody, blending their music in perfect harmony. The crowd clapped and cheered, as the couple exchanged garlands of flowers, symbolizing their union.

And so, Armita and Bharadwaja were married, surrounded by friends and family from both cultures.

Baguhara felt joy, his eyes bright with pride. "My daughter's marriage will be a symbol of light." he announced.

The marriage of Princess Armita and Bharadwaja marked the beginning of a new era of peace and harmony between the Harappans and Aryans. It showed that even the most divided of people could come together, and that love, and unity could conquer even the greatest of differences.

* * *

Years passed, and Princess Armita gave birth to a beautiful baby boy, Maharudra. He was the culmination of their love and the symbol of their union. Armita and Bharadwaja cherished every moment with their son, watching him grow and flourish with joy.

"You are the light of our lives, Maharudra," Princess Armita said, holding him close.

"And you are the future of our people," added Bharadwaja, smiling.

Baguhara felt immense joy and pride with Maharudra's birth, as Armita was his only child. He had always wanted a grandchild to carry on his legacy, and now his dream had come true. He showered Maharudra with love and affection, spending hours playing with him, teaching him the ways of the kingdom, and sharing his wisdom.

* * *

As Maharudra grew up, he was surrounded by the love and wisdom of both his parents and his grandfather. He was taught the importance of unity, compassion, and strength, and he absorbed these lessons with a curious mind.

"Grandfather, what's the secret to a happy and prosperous life?" Maharudra asked Baguhara as they walked in the gardens.

"Harmony and cooperation, my prince," Baguhara replied with a warm smile. "Unity is the key to success and happiness. Never forget that our strength lies in working together."

"I will not forget, grandfather," Maharudra replied.

"And always remember, Maharudra, that a true leader is one who leads with wisdom and integrity," Baguhara added. "Don't forget to cherish and protect your people, and always strive to build a brighter future for the society."

"I will, grandfather," Maharudra said, his voice filled with conviction.

"What's our greatest challenge, Grandfather?" Maharudra asked another day.

"Division and conflict, Maharudra," Baguhara replied, his voice firm. "We must always stand united against forces that seek to tear us apart."

"I understand, Grandfather," Maharudra said, his eyes determined. "But what about the Aryans? Do they pose any problem to our kingdom?"

"The Aryans are complex, Maharudra," Baguhara replied thoughtfully. "Some may pose a threat, but others are our allies. We must be cautious, yet also seek common ground to work with them."

"But Grandfather, what about their beliefs?" Maharudra asked.

"Ah, a good question," Baguhara replied. "The Aryans have different beliefs, but that doesn't mean they're incompatible with ours. We can learn from each other and find common ground. Understanding and respect can bridge any divide."

"I see," Maharudra said, thinking deeply. "But what about their varna system? Don't they discriminate?"

"Yes, some do," Baguhara replied seriously. "But we mustn't judge all Aryans by the actions of a few. Many reject such biases and value all people, regardless of social status or background."

Maharudra nodded, his mind filled with questions and thoughts. "I will remember that grandfather. Thank you for your wisdom."

* * *

The kingdom flourished for many years, its people living in harmony and prosperity, under the wise and visionary leadership of its ruler Baguhara.

As Baguhara's life came to a close, a new generation had risen to carry on his legacy, and his grandson Maharudra, the son of Princess Armita and Bharadwaja, took up the reins of power.

The day of Maharudra's coronation was a grand and solemn occasion, with the entire kingdom gathering to witness the dawn of a new era. The sun rose over the palace, casting a warm orange hue over the assembled crowd, as Maharudra, elegant in his royal attire, ascended to the throne.

Armita and Bharadwaja, seated beside him, beamed with pride, their hearts overflowing with joy and gratitude. They had raised a son who was not only wise and just, but also strong and compassionate, with a heart full of love for his people.

As Maharudra accepted the crown, a symbol of his authority and responsibility, the crowd erupted in cheers and applause, their faces filled with hope and expectation.

Armita and Bharadwaja exchanged a glance, their eyes brimming with tears of happiness. They had always known that their son was destined for greatness, and now, as they saw him sitting on the throne, they knew that their dream had come true.

"We did it" Armita whispered, her voice trembling with emotion. "We raised a king who will bring peace and prosperity to our people."

Bharadwaja nodded; his face radiant with pride. "We did, my love. And we will always be proud of our son, who has become a true leader."

As the coronation ceremony came to a close, Maharudra stood up, his voice ringing out across the kingdom. "My dear people," he said, his words filled with passion and conviction. "I promise to rule with wisdom and compassion, to protect and serve you, and to bring peace and prosperity to our beloved kingdom. Let us work together to build a brighter future, and let our unity and harmony be an example to the world."

The crowd roared with approval, and Armita and Bharadwaja smiled, knowing that their son was truly a king for the ages.

As the years passed, the once-rigid social boundaries began to blur, and people from all walks of life came together in celebration of their shared humanity. Intermarriage became a powerful symbol of the region's newfound harmony, as families from both societies merged their traditions and created a vibrant, diverse culture.

"We are no longer divided," said King Maharudra, as he looked out upon his people.

"We are one, united in our quest for peace and prosperity."

And so, the Harappans and Aryans forged a lasting legacy, their once-divided societies now a symbol of the human spirit's remarkable ability to heal, unite, and overcome even the most daunting challenges. But, as the sands of time whisper secrets to the wind, one wonders... did the shadows of the past truly dissipate, or did they merely hide, waiting for the perfect moment to strike?

Chapter Thirteen

The Embrace of Pashupathi

As Aryans continued to learn from and integrate with the Harappans, they became increasingly drawn to the powerful and complex deity, Pashupathi, later known as Shiva. This mighty god was depicted as a majestic figure with multiple arms, each representing a different aspect of the universe. His fierce gaze was said to pierce through the veil of ignorance, revealing the ultimate truth to those who sought it.

Pashupathi was the lord of the cosmos, the master of time and space, and the guardian of the cycles of life and death. His sacred symbol, the trident, represented the three aspects of the universe: creation, preservation, and destruction. His cosmic dance, the Tandava, was said to balance the forces of the universe, maintaining harmony and order in eternity.

As the seasons passed, Armita, Bharadwaja, and Varuna's time on this earth came to an end. They departed, leaving behind a legacy of compassion and wisdom. Their memory faded with the passing years, but the impact of their efforts to save the Harappans lived on, a gentle breeze that lingered through the ages.

With a new chapter in Harappan-Aryan cooperation, a fresh dawn broke, carrying with it the promise of a new future and the echoes of a rich heritage.

* * *

Meanwhile, as the soft moonlight cast a silver glow over the bustling city of Rakhigarhi, illuminating the crowded streets and marketplaces, a young Aryan warrior named Indrasena rose to prominence. His piercing brown eyes seemed to bore into those he met, and his broad shoulders and muscular physique spoke of a strength forged in the fire of battle. His sharp jawline and prominent nose gave him a resolute appearance, a true warrior of the Kshatriya. And in his veins flowed the true Kshatriya blood, a warrior's spirit that would never surrender, never yield.

Even as a child, Indrasena had been consumed by an insatiable ambition, a burning desire to achieve greatness and leave his mark on the world. He would spend hours poring over the ancient texts, devouring stories of legendary heroes and mighty warriors, and dreaming of the day he would join their ranks. His parents and teachers would often marvel at his focus and determination, and his peers would look on in awe as he effortlessly bested them in every competition, every challenge.

As a member of the Kshatriya family, Indrasena was born into a life of privilege and duty. His family was respected and influential, and he was trained from a young age in the art of combat and leadership. But Indrasena was not content to simply follow in the footsteps of his ancestors; he was determined to forge his own path, to carve out his own destiny.

One day, while on a solo hunting trip, Indrasena stumbled upon a stranger who would change his life forever. The stranger, a wise and aged Harappan sage named Nagashourya, revealed himself to be a master of the ancient arts. He saw potential in the young warrior and took him under his wing, teaching him the secrets of combat, strategy, and leadership.

"Indrasena, my young friend," Nagashourya said, his voice low and soothing, "you have a fire within you, a flame that burns bright with potential. But to truly harness your power, you must learn to control your emotions, to quiet the mind and listen to the heart."

"I am eager to learn, Nagashourya," Indrasena replied, his eyes wide with enthusiasm. "Teach me the secrets of the ancient arts, that I may become a true warrior and leader."

Nagashourya smiled, his eyes twinkling with wisdom. "The secrets are not mine to give, Indrasena. They are yours to discover. But I will guide you on your journey, and share with you the wisdom of the ages."

Under Nagashourya's guidance, Indrasena flourished. He learned to harness his strength, speed, and agility, becoming a formidable force on the battlefield. He also developed a deep understanding of the world, its complexities, and its many cultures. Nagashourya's wisdom and mentorship helped Indrasena become an even greater leader, respected by his peers and admired by his people.

* * *

Years passed, and Indrasena's reputation grew. With Nagashourya's help, he has become a trusted military leader under the king Maharudra.

One day, Indrasena's curiosity led him to the ancient temple of Shiva, where he sought guidance from the wise Harappan sage, Nagashourya.

The temple of Shiva was a majestic structure, its walls were carved with intricate depictions of various animals, each one symbolizing a different aspect of existence. Elephants, with their wrinkled skin and tusks, represented wisdom and strength. Tigers, with their fierce eyes and sharp claws, represented courage and power. And unicorns, with their shimmering coats and horns, represented purity and magic.

As Indrasena entered the temple, the air enveloped him, heavy with the sweet, pungent aroma of sandalwood incense, transporting him to a realm of spiritual contemplation. The sound of chanting priests filled the air, their voices rising and falling in a soothing melody.

Nagashourya, a descendant of the Harappan family, was born and raised in the city of Harappa. His slender figure and piercing eyes seemed to hold the weight of centuries, his long white hair a badge of his wisdom. His gentle smile put even the most skeptical of souls at ease, and his voice was like a soothing gust on a hot day.

"Ah, Indrasena, my young friend," Nagashourya said, his voice low and soothing. "I see you have finally understood the true meaning of Shiva." His eyes crinkled at the corners as he smiled, his nod of approval accompanied by a gentle incline of his head.

Indrasena leaned forward; his eyes gleaming with newfound understanding. "Yes, Nagashourya.

I have come to realize that Shiva is not just a god, but a symbol of the eternal cycle of creation and destruction." His voice was filled with conviction, his words spoken with a sense of wonder.

Nagashourya' s eyes shone with approval. "You have indeed, Indrasena. And with this understanding comes great responsibility. You must use your knowledge to maintain balance and harmony in the world." His voice was like a gentle breeze, carrying the weight of wisdom and experience.

As they delved deeper into the mysteries of Shiva, they began to see the world in a new light. They realized that their conquests and victories were not the only measures of success, and that true wisdom lay in living in harmony with the natural world and with each other.

"The Gods are not just distant beings, but aspects of ourselves," said Indrasena, his eyes gleaming with newfound understanding. "Shiva is the destroyer, but also the transformer. He reminds us that change is the only constant in life." But in that moment, Indrasena didn't realize the true nature of fleeting mind and the change it can bring upon him.

"Indeed," said Nagashourya. "And it is our ability to adapt and evolve that will determine our true strength as a people." His words were like a gentle rain, nourishing the soil of their minds.

Meanwhile, Aryan priests saw their own deity Rudra in Shiva as a reflection of strength, courage, destruction, and the cyclical nature of life and death. They recognized that Pashupathi embodied the same qualities they revered in Rudra: the fierce protector, the destroyer of evil, and the transformer of existence.

As they continued to explore the mysteries of Pashupathi, the Aryans discovered the rich symbolism and mythology surrounding this powerful deity. They learned of his role as the patron of yoga and meditation, guiding seekers on the path to enlightenment and self-realization.

And so, the worship of Pashupathi, or Shiva, became an integral part of the Aryan spiritual tradition, a celebration of the fusion of cultures and the universal quest for understanding and connection with the divine.

Chapter Fourteen

The Epic of Rama

In the golden age of King Maharudra's rule, arts and literature flourished, and the land of the Harappans was filled with the sweet sounds of music, poetry, and storytelling. It was during this time that a great epic was born - the Ramayana. Written by the sage, Valmiki, it told the story of Rama, a king of unparalleled virtue and courage.

"Valmiki, your words have brought Rama to life," said Indrasena, his voice filled with awe. "But why did you choose to tell the story of Rama now?"

"Because, my lord," replied Valmiki, "Rama's story is not just a tale of heroism, but a reminder of our shared humanity. His struggles and triumphs are a reflection of our own challenges and achievements we are facing today. Rama's unwavering dedication to duty, his unshakeable integrity, and his boundless compassion are an inspiration to us all. His passion for his people, his desire to protect and serve them, is a quality that we can all strive for."

"And what of Sita, his queen?" asked Nagashourya, his eyes sparkling with curiosity. "Her story is one of courage and loyalty, a true embodiment of the Harappan spirit."

"Indeed," said Valmiki. "Sita's character is a gesture of the strength and resilience of women in our society. Her devotion to Rama is a reminder of the power of love and commitment."

As the Ramayana spread throughout the land, it became a symbol of unity and shared heritage between the Aryans and Harappans. Both cultures claimed Rama as their own, and in doing so, found common ground.

The Harappans saw in Rama a reflection of their own values - courage, honor, and loyalty. The Aryans saw in him a symbol of their own struggles and triumphs. And in Sita, they saw a beautiful example of the strength and grace of women.

"Rama's passion for his people is truly inspiring," said Indrasena. "He sacrificed so much for their benefit, and yet he never expected anything in return."

"Yes," said Valmiki. "Rama's selflessness is a quality that we can all learn from. He put the needs of his people before his own, and in doing so, he became a true hero."

"I am so grateful to have heard this story," said Nagashourya. "It has reminded me of the importance of compassion and service to others."

Temples and shrines dedicated to Rama began to appear throughout the land, and his image became a ubiquitous presence in daily life. People would offer prayers and perform rituals in his name, seeking guidance and protection.

The worship of Rama became a natural extension of their shared culture, a way to honor the values and principles that had brought them together. It was as if Rama's spirit had become a guardian of their unity, a reminder of the power of courage, compassion, and duty.

The Ramayana had brought them together, reminding them that their stories were not so different after all. And in that realization, they found a lasting peace, one that would endure for generations to come.

Chapter Fifteen

A New Era of Cooperation

"King Maharudra, your wisdom has brought our people together," said Indrasena, his voice filled with gratitude. "We Aryans have much to learn from your wisdom and experience."

"This is a new era of cooperation," said Nagashourya, his voice filled with hope. "Together, we can build a brighter future, one that honors our shared humanity."

"Indeed," said Indrasena. "And it is our ability to see beyond our differences that will determine our true strength as a people."

"We have much to learn from each other," said King Maharudra. "Let us continue to exchange ideas and traditions, that we may grow stronger together."

"Agreed," said Indrasena. "And let us not forget the power of Rama's story, which has brought us together in this new era of cooperation."

"Yes," said Nagashourya. "Rama's legacy will live on, a reminder of our shared cultural heritage and our ability to come together in the face of adversity."

One day, Indrasena approached King Maharudra with a respectful gesture. "Your Majesty, I hope I am not being too forward, but I had an idea that I believe could bring great benefit to our people."

Maharudra looked at him thoughtfully. "Speak, Indrasena. What is it?"

"I was thinking that perhaps we could perform a Yaga, a sacred ritual, to ensure the well-being of our people and also the victory in the conquests to come" Indrasena suggested.

Maharudra furrowed his brow, considering the idea. He thanked Indrasena for his suggestion and told him that he would think about it.

Weeks passed, and Indrasena waited patiently for Maharudra's response. Finally, the king called for him once again.

"Indrasena, I have thought about your suggestion, and I have decided to agree to perform the Yaga," Maharudra said, his expression thoughtful. "It may indeed forge a stronger bond between our people and the Aryans and bring us victory in our conquests."

Indrasena's face lit up with a smile. "Thank you, Your Majesty! I will see to the preparations immediately."

The preparations for the Yaga began in earnest, with Indrasena overseeing the arrangements. Maharudra, meanwhile, spent his days in contemplation, preparing himself for the ritual.

As the day of the Yaga approached, the city was filled with excitement and anticipation. The people had heard of the ritual's power to bring victory and prosperity, and they eagerly awaited its performance.

Finally, the day arrived, and the city's central square was filled with people from all walks of life. Maharudra and Indrasena stood at the forefront, surrounded by priests and dignitaries.

The Yaga was performed on a grand scale, with elaborate preparations and rituals. A large sacrificial altar was built, adorned with flowers, incense, and sacred symbols.

King Maharudra, Indrasena, and the Aryan priests donned their ceremonial attire, complete with sacred threads and gemstone-encrusted crowns.

As the sun rose over the city, the Yaga began with the chanting of sacred mantras and the lighting of the sacrificial fire. The Aryan priests led the chanting, their voices rising and falling in a soothing cadence:

"Agni Mimile Purohitam...

Yajnaasya Deva Rtvijam...

Hotaram Ratna Dhetam...

(Agni, the divine priest, the sacrificer, the bearer of oblations...)"

"Vishwamitra Ayushh Te...

Agni Shri Te Kuru Prachetah...

Vishwa Deva Asya Vishiti...

(May Vishwamitra grant you long life... May Agni make your mind pure... May all gods dwell in this sacrifice...)"

King Maharudra and the priests offered oblations of ghee, grains, and precious herbs into the flames, accompanied by the sweet fragrance of burning incense.

The ritual continued with the sacrifice of sacred animals, symbolizing the surrender of ego and the selfless pursuit of knowledge. The priests chanted hymns and sang sacred songs, while the people gathered around the altar, watching in awe and reverence.

As the Yaga reached its climax, King Maharudra and Indrasena jointly offered a final oblation, a golden vessel filled with sacred water, into the fiery depths of the altar.

"Om Shantih, Shantih, Shantih, Om" chanted the priests, as the people erupted in cheers and applause, knowing that their unity and cooperation had been sealed in the eyes of the gods.

As a result, a vibrant cultural exchange flourished between the two societies. Harappan and Aryan scholars collaborated on new texts, blending their knowledge and ideas. Harappan artists and Aryan craftsmen worked together, creating beautiful works that reflected the best of both cultures.

But, as the celebrations continue and the people rejoice, a whisper begins to circulate, hinting that the tides of time are about to shift in unexpected ways. The Harappans were living in the moment, unaware that their life was about to be turned upside down.

Chapter Sixteen

The Aryan Conquest

With their newfound unity and cultural exchange, the Harappan-Aryan alliance became a formidable force. They set their sights on the surrounding kingdoms, seeking to expand their borders and spread their influence.

"King Maharudra, our armies are ready to march," said Indrasena, his voice filled with determination. "Together, we will conquer the surrounding kingdoms and bring them under our rule."

"I agree, Indrasena," replied King Maharudra, his eyes gleaming with strategic thinking.

"But we must do so with wisdom and justice. We must show the people of these kingdoms that our rule is fair and benevolent."

As they marched towards the neighboring kingdoms, they were met with varying degrees of resistance. Some kingdoms surrendered quickly, while others put up a fierce fight.

"We will not be defeated!" cried the king of the neighboring kingdom of Kalinga. "We will fight to the last man!"

"You are brave, King Kalinga," replied Indrasena, his voice filled with respect. "But bravery must be tempered with wisdom. Surrender now and spare your people the bloodshed."

The armies of the Harappan-Aryan alliance marched forward, their banners waving in the wind. The sound of drums and trumpets filled the air, and the ground shook beneath the hooves of their horses and the feet of their elephants.

As they approached the kingdom of Kalinga, they were met with fierce resistance. The king of Kalinga, determined to defend his kingdom, led his army into battle.

The two armies clashed in a frenzy of swords and spears, the sound of clashing bronze metal and the cries of the wounded filling the air. Indrasena, his sword flashing in the sunlight, led the charge against the kingdom of Kalinga.

King Maharudra, his elephant trumpeting a fierce battle cry, followed close behind, his eyes fixed on the enemy lines. Nagashourya, his wise eyes scanning the battlefield, directed the troops with strategic expertise.

As the battle raged on, King Maharudra fought with determination. His sword sliced through the Kalinga warriors with deadly finesse. But fate had other plans. A stray arrow, shot by a Kalinga archer, struck Maharudra in the chest. It pierced his armor lodging deep in his heart. Maharudra's elephant, sensing the distress, let out a mournful cry and knelt beside him. He was taken to his chambers immediately by his soldiers, where he was treated by the royal healers.

Indrasena and Nagashourya, filled with pain and determination, took up the mantle of leadership, vowing to avenge their wounded king and secure victory for their people.

With Nagashourya's guidance, Indrasena led the charge against the Kalinga army. The war was fierce and long, but Indrasena's bravery and tactical prowess ultimately led to victory.

* * *

As the days passed, Maharudra's wound deepened. His vision blurring, he looked up at Indrasena and Nagashourya, his eyes filled with a deep sadness.

"My friends...protect our people...do not let our alliance...fade into darkness..." he whispered. With those final words, King Maharudra's eyes closed, leaving Harappa in the hands of Indrasena and Nagashourya.

The people of Harappa mourned the loss of their beloved king, their voices filled with grief and sorrow.

"He was a just and fair ruler," said one Harappan, tears streaming down her face. "He brought peace and prosperity to our city."

"I will never forget his wisdom and guidance," said another, his voice cracking with emotion. "He was a true leader and a friend to all."

As the news of Maharudra's passing spread, the city of Harappa came together to pay their respects to their fallen king.

With the kingdom in mourning, Nagashourya knew that a new leader had to be appointed to guide the alliance forward. He looked at Indrasena, who had stood by Maharudra's side throughout the conquests. Indrasena's bravery, strategic thinking, and loyalty made him the ideal candidate to succeed Maharudra.

"May Indrasena continue Maharudra's legacy and lead us to even greater heights," said Nagashourya, his voice filled with hope and determination. "May Maharudra's memory be a blessing to us all."

The people of Harappa nodded in agreement, and Nagashourya continued, "Let us crown Indrasena as our new king, that he may lead us forward in these uncertain times."

The people of Harappa mourned the loss of their king, but they also looked to the future, ready to face whatever challenges lay ahead under the leadership of Indrasena.

* * *

Indrasena, with a heavy heart, accepted the crown. His parents felt that he was destined to be the king. The coronation of Indrasena was welcomed by Harappans with mixed feelings. Streets were decorated with colorful artwork and mesmerizing sounds of drums and trumpets filled the ears. Elephants, horses, and chariots paraded through the city with riders waving banners and singing songs in praise of the new king.

Indrasena was anointed with sacred oils and crowned with a golden diadem. The high priest of the temple, opulent in his golden robes, performed the rituals with great solemnity, and the people of Harappa cheered and chanted as Indrasena was proclaimed as the new king.

At first, Indrasena's rule was met with optimism. He made grand promises to his people, vowing to expand the empire's borders and bring prosperity to all. He was charismatic and confident, and his people believed in him.

However, as time passed, subtle changes began to creep into Indrasena's behavior. His smile, once warm and inclusive, grew tighter and more calculating. His eyes, once bright with vision, took on a cold, hard glint. He began to surround himself with yes-men and flatterers, who praised his every move and never dared to question his decisions.

Indrasena began to appoint more Aryans to positions of power, slowly marginalizing the Harappans from leadership roles. He also started to promote Aryan customs and traditions, while gently discouraging Harappan practices.

His desire for power and recognition consumed him slowly. He became obsessed with becoming the greatest king of all lands, and his rule grew increasingly authoritarian. He taxed his people heavily, using the wealth to fund his military conquests and grandiose projects. He silenced any opposition, and his people lived in fear of his displeasure.

Nagashourya, the wise strategist, watched with growing concern as his friend and leader descended into madness.

"This is not the Indrasena I once knew," Nagashourya thought to himself. "He was once a brave and inclusive leader, but now he is consumed by his desire for power and recognition. I fear for the future of our alliance, and for the people of Harappa."

As he thought to himself, Nagashourya couldn't help but miss the wise and just leadership of King Maharudra, who had always put the needs of his people before his own ambition. He remembered the king's kind heart, his fair and compassionate rule, and his ability to bring people together.

Nagashourya sighed, knowing that those days were gone, and that Indrasena's rule was a far cry from the wise leadership of King Maharudra. He tried to reason with Indrasena, to bring him back from the brink of destruction, but the king would not listen.

"Indrasena, my friend, please reconsider your actions," Nagashourya said, his voice laced with a hint of sadness. "Your people are suffering; your land is burning. Is this truly the legacy you wish to leave behind?"

"Enough, Nagashourya!" Indrasena snapped; his face twisted in anger. "You are weak, always cautioning me to hold back. But I will not be held back. I am the greatest king this land has ever known, and I will do whatever it takes to maintain my power."

Nagashourya sighed, his eyes filled with a deep sorrow. "I fear for our alliance, Indrasena. We were once a beacon of hope, a great example of cooperation.

Now we are a mere shadow of our former selves. Is this truly what you desire?"

Indrasena turned away, his expression unyielding. "You are no longer needed, Nagashourya. Your counsel is no longer required. Leave me, and do not return until I summon you."

And with that, Nagashourya was dismissed, left to watch from afar as the empire crumbled, its people suffering under the weight of Indrasena's ambition.

As the empire continued to expand, a sense of unease began to grow among the people. The Harappan-Aryan alliance, once a symbol of unity and cooperation, began to show signs of strain. The Aryans, with their dominant military power, began to assert their control over the Harappans, and the once-equal partnership began to fray.

The Aryans started to enforce the Varna system, a rigid social hierarchy that divided people into four categories: Brahmins, Kshatriyas, Vaishyas, and Shudras. The Harappans, who had never known such a system, began to resent the Varna system that was imposed on them.

"Why must we be bound by these arbitrary divisions?" asked a young Harappan. "We were once equals, and now we are treated as inferiors."

"The Varna system is the natural order of things," replied an Aryan priest. "It is the will of the gods."

Meanwhile, King Indrasena, who had once fought for the united Harappans and Aryans, began to exclude Harappans from joining the combined military. He claimed that Harappans were not equivalent to Aryan Kshatriya and therefore did not possess the necessary martial prowess.

But some Harappans were not convinced. They began to see the Varna system as a tool of oppression, a way for the Aryans to maintain their power and control over the empire.

In hushed tones, the Harappans started to talk about Indrasena. "He is a tyrant, consumed by his own ambition," they whispered.

"He cares not for the welfare of our people, only for his own power and glory."

"He is a shadow of his former self," others said. "He was once a brave and inclusive leader, but now he is a mere tool of the ruling elite."

"I fear for our future," said an elderly Harappan, his eyes filled with sadness. "We are losing our way of life, our culture, our traditions. We are becoming strangers in our own land."

The people of Harappa began to lose hope, their spirits crushed by the weight of Indrasena's rule. They longed for the wise leadership of King Maharudra. But Maharudra was gone, and Indrasena's rule seemed to have no end in sight.

As the fate of the Harappans teeters on the edge of uncertainty, their future plunged into darkness and despair. Harappans once proud and vibrant, are now struggling to survive under the burden of oppression.

Chapter Seventeen

The Aryan Identity

As the Harappan-Aryan empire continued to expand, a curious phenomenon emerged. More and more people, regardless of their actual heritage, began to identify as Aryan. The term had become synonymous with cultural superiority, military prowess, and intellectual excellence.

Many people started claiming Aryan identity out of fear - fear of being seen as inferior, fear of being left behind, or fear of being marginalized. They believed that identifying as Aryan would guarantee them a place in the empire's hierarchy, and so they adopted the label with enthusiasm. Some even went so far as to fabricate Aryan lineage, inventing stories of noble ancestors and illustrious family histories. Others simply adopted Aryan customs and traditions, hoping to blend in with the dominant culture.

"I am Aryan, praise me!" declared a young warrior, his eyes blazing with pride.

"But what does it mean to be Aryan?" asked a wise old scholar, his voice laced with skepticism. "Is it not just a label, a way to distinguish oneself from others?"

"It means to be the best, to be superior," replied the warrior, his chest puffed out. "We Aryans have achieved greatness, and our culture is the pinnacle of human achievement."

"Ah but is that not a dangerous notion?" asked the scholar, his eyes narrowing. "To think oneself superior to others simply because of one's identity? It leads to exclusion, to division, and to the erasure of other cultures."

"Exclusion?" repeated the warrior, his brow furrowed. "What do you mean? We Aryans are the most inclusive people; we welcome everyone into our fold... as long as they wear our tradition of clothes and follow the rituals."

"Inclusive?" asked the scholar, his voice laced with irony. "You mean, as long as they adopt your culture, your language, and your customs? That is not inclusivity, that is cultural imperialism."

"I had not thought of that," the warrior said, his voice barely above a whisper.

"Exactly," said the scholar, his voice filled with wisdom. "Identity can be a powerful force, but it must be wielded with care. We must not let it divide us, but rather unite us in our shared humanity."

The warrior nodded; his eyes filled with a newfound understanding.

"Thank you," he said, his voice filled with gratitude. "I see now that my pride was misplaced. I will strive to be a better Aryan, one who celebrates our diversity, and not just our dominance."

The scholar smiled; his eyes filled with warmth.

"That is the first step towards true greatness," he said. "To recognize the value of others, and to strive for inclusivity, rather than exclusivity."

* * *

But as the days passed, some Harappans grew more and more restless. They felt that their culture was being erased, their traditions forgotten, and their people marginalized. They began to whisper among themselves, their voices filled with anger and frustration.

"We're not allowed to speak our language in public anymore," said one. "They say it's not civilized enough."

"They're replacing our temples with Aryan statues," said another. "Our gods are being forgotten."

"They're forcing us to wear Aryan clothes and adopt their rituals," said a third. "We're losing our identity."

They felt a sadness in their hearts, a sense of losing their way. "We're not the same people we used to be," they thought. "We're fading away." This thought scared them, and they knew they had to do something to preserve their culture and identity.

"We can't stay here anymore," they said quietly. "We have to leave before we disappear completely."

And so, the Harappan Exodus was about to begin. A great migration of people, leaving behind the empire that had once been their home, in search of a new land where they could preserve their culture and their identity.

The warrior and the scholar, unaware of the impending departure, continued to discuss the intricacies of identity and culture, but the fate of the Harappans was already sealed.

Chapter Eighteen

The Harappan Exodus

As the Aryan identity became the dominant cultural force, some Harappans began to feel disillusioned. They felt that their own unique culture and traditions were being erased, absorbed into the larger Aryan identity.

The Harappans knew that they couldn't stay and watch their identity fade away. They needed to find a new home, a place where they could be free to be themselves, to speak their language, to practice their traditions, and to worship their gods. They dreamt of a place where they could be proud of who they were, without fear of persecution or erasure.

A group of Harappans, led by a wise and aged scholar named Nannay, decided to take a stand. They longed for autonomy, for the freedom to preserve their own way of life, untainted by the influences of the empire. They also deeply resented the Varna system, which they saw as a tool of oppression, forcing them into rigid social hierarchies and limiting their potential.

"We are not just Shudras or Vaishyas," Nannay declared. "We are Harappans, with our own rich heritage and customs. We will not be bound by these arbitrary hierarchies that divide us based on what we do."

They began to secretly gather like-minded individuals, sharing their concerns and fears about the erosion of their cultural heritage. Nannay, with his deep understanding of Harappan heritage and traditions, became the leader of this quiet rebellion.

"We must act now, before it's too late," Nannay urged his fellow Harappans. "We must preserve our language, our customs, our art. We must keep our identity alive and reject the shackles of the Varna system."

The group started to organize, forming a network of hidden communities and secret meeting places. They shared stories, songs, and poems, keeping their cultural traditions alive in the shadows.

But their actions did not go unnoticed. The Aryan authorities, suspicious of any dissent, arrested Nannay and threw him into prison.

Indrasena, the Aryan king, sneered at Nannay's capture. "You are a fool, Nannay," he said. "You will never succeed in your rebellion. The empire is too strong, too powerful. You will rot in prison, and your people will forget you."

But Nannay was not the one to give up easily. He used his knowledge of the prison's layout, gained from his years of studying the empire's architecture, to plan his escape. One night, under the cover of darkness, he slipped out of his cell and made his way to the prison gates.

As he reached the gates, he heard the sound of footsteps echoing through the corridor. The guards had discovered his escape and were closing in on him. Nannay's heart raced as he pushed open the gates and sprinted out into the night.

He ran through the winding streets of the city, the guards hot on his heels. He dodged and weaved, using his knowledge of the city's alleys and side streets to evade his pursuers. But just as he thought he had shaken them off, he heard the sound of horses' hooves behind him.

Nannay turned to see a group of mounted guards bearing down on him, their swords drawn. He knew he couldn't outrun them, so he did the only thing he could think of - he leapt into the nearby river, plunging into the cold waters.

The guards reined in their horses, shouting and pointing at the spot where Nannay had disappeared. But Nannay was a strong swimmer, and he knew the river like the back of his hand. He swam underwater, his heart pounding in his chest, until he reached the other side.

Exhausted and shivering, he pulled himself out of the water and looked around. He was in a deserted alley, the city's buildings looming above him like giants. He knew he had to keep moving, so he stumbled forward, his eyes fixed on the horizon.

Finally, after what seemed like hours of walking, he saw a figure waiting for him in the shadows. It was one of his fellow rebels, who had been sent to guide him to safety.

"Nannay, we thought we had lost you," the man said, embracing him warmly.

"I will never be lost," Nannay replied, his eyes bright with determination. "I will always find a way to fight for our people, for our culture, and for our freedom."

As the tensions mounted, Nannay knew that their struggle was far from over. He vowed to continue fighting for the rights of his people, to keep their culture and traditions alive, and to dismantle the oppressive Varna system.

"We cannot let our culture be consumed by the empire," said Nannay, his eyes burning with determination. "We must take a stand, for our ancestors and for our children."

"But where will we go?" asked a young Harappan, his voice trembling with fear. "The forests are treacherous, and we have no home beyond the empire."

"We will find a way," said Nannay, his voice filled with conviction. "We will find a new home, where we can live in peace, and preserve our way of life."

After much discussion, the group decided to move south to the lands beyond the empire's reach. They had heard of a fertile valley, where the rivers flowed pure, and the land was rich with resources.

To reach this new home, they would have to cross the Deccan Plateau, a vast and unforgiving landscape of rocky hills and dry rivers. But they were determined to succeed, and so they set out on their journey.

As they prepared to leave, they couldn't help but feel a sense of loss and longing. They remembered the days when their culture was thriving, when their language and traditions were celebrated, and when their gods were revered. They recalled the vibrant markets, the colorful festivals, and the rich stories that were passed down through generations.

The Harappans who remained behind gathered to bid them farewell. Tears flowed freely, as friends and family said their goodbyes. Nagashourya couldn't shake off the feeling that he was abandoning his people, his culture, and his own sense of purpose. He wondered if he would ever find the strength to resist the empire's oppressive rule, or if he would remain a silent witness to the erasure of his people's identity.

"I will never forget you," said Nagashourya, his voice choked with emotion. "You are the keepers of our culture, and I will always be grateful for your bravery."

"We will never forget you either," said Nannay, his eyes flooded with tears. "You are our brothers and sisters, and we will carry you in our hearts always."

Nannay was accompanied by his wife, two daughters, and his parents. His family remained a source of strength and inspiration for him throughout their journey.

As they set out, Nannay's daughters clung to him, their faces etched with worry and fear. "Father, will we ever find a new home?" one of them asked, her voice trembling.

"We will, my child," Nannay replied, his voice filled with conviction. "We will find a place where we can live in peace and preserve our way of life."

"But what if we get hurt, or lost, or..." the other daughter's voice trailed off, her eyes welling up with tears.

Nannay embraced his daughters, holding them close to his heart. "We will face challenges, yes, but we will face them together. We will support each other, and we will never give up. We are Harappans, and we are strong and resilient."

And with that, the Harappans set out on their journey, disappearing into the unknown lands beyond the empire. They traveled for many moons, facing countless challenges and dangers along the way. They crossed the Deccan Plateau, braving the harsh sun and the dry, barren landscape. The rocky hills and dry rivers stretched out before them like an endless desert, and the group struggled to find food and water.

As they traversed this unforgiving terrain, some of the Harappans began to fall ill, weakened by the harsh climate and the scarcity of resources. The elderly and the young were the first to succumb, their bodies worn down by the relentless journey. Nannay and his followers did their best to care for them, but despite their efforts, some of their companions passed away.

The group mourned each loss, their grief and fatigue threatening to overwhelm them. But they pressed on, driven by their determination to find a new home and preserve their culture. They shared what little food and water they had and supported each other through the darkest moments.

Finally, after many long and difficult months, they reached the fertile valley and began to build a new home. The ones who remained behind whispered the stories of their bravery, of their determination to preserve their way of life.

"They are heroes, not cowards," said Nagashourya, his voice filled with admiration.

"They have shown us that even in the face of overwhelming power, the human spirit can find a way to persevere."

But as the days passed, the reality of their departure set in. The empire barely noticed their absence, and the Harappans who remained behind were left to wonder if they had made a mistake.

And so, the Harappan Exodus became a legend, a symbol of resistance against cultural assimilation, a reminder that even in the darkest of times, there is always hope for a brighter future. But for those who remained behind, it was also a reminder of the pain of separation, and the uncertainty of what lay ahead.

The Harappans who ventured south embarked on a new chapter in their lives, building resilient kingdoms and forging a vibrant culture. Their new homeland became known as Dravida, and they came to be called Dravidians. Though they never forgot their Harappan heritage and the ancient civilization that once flourished along the Sindhu River, they also embraced their new identity, shaped by the challenges and triumphs in their new homeland.

Chapter Nineteen

The Aryan Military Might

As the Harappan Exodus faded into memory, the Aryan king Indrasena continued to consolidate his power. He turned his attention to developing the military, seeking to create an unstoppable force that would secure dominance for generations to come.

"We must build an army that will be remembered for eternity," said Indrasena, to his generals, his voice echoing through the throne room, which was adorned with intricate carvings and tapestries. "An army that will strike fear into the hearts of our enemies, an army that will be the stuff of legend."

"We will need the strongest soldiers, the best tactics, and the finest weapons," replied one of his generals, his eyes gleaming with ambition, his armor reflecting in the sunlight that streamed through the windows. "But we must also remember the importance of discipline and loyalty. Our soldiers must be conditioned to follow orders without question, unstoppable and unyielding."

"I agree," said Indrasena, his expression cold and calculating, his eyes narrowed in determination.

"We will train them to be fearless and relentless. And with our new crafts, such as cavalry and archers, we will be unbeatable. Our armor and weapons will be forged from the strongest materials, crafted with meticulousness, and shine with a fierce light."

The Aryan army became a well-oiled machine, with each soldier trained to perfection. They marched into battle with precision, their armor and weapons polished to a high sheen, their war elephants massive and fearsome, trained to charge into battle with deadly dexterity. The air was filled with the sound of weapons clashing and the smell of sweat and metal as they battled.

Indrasena's military campaigns were swift and decisive, as he conquered kingdom after kingdom in a span of just a few years. He led his army across the land, leaving a trail of defeated enemies and subjugated peoples in his wake. His war elephants trampled the fields and cities of his foes, their tusks glowing in the sunlight as they charged into battle.

His archers rained arrows down upon his enemies, their bows singing with a deadly music. His cavalry rode down the fleeing soldiers, their swords raised high as they cut down any who dared to resist.

The army of elephants was a marvel of training and strategy. The elephants were adorned with intricate decorations, their tusks sharpened to deadly points. The soldiers rode on their backs, armed with spears and swords, ready to strike at a moment's notice.

The cavalry was equally impressive, with horses bred for speed and strength. The Aryans had developed a new style of riding, using stirrups and saddles to give their soldiers greater control and mobility. The horses were trained to respond to every command, to charge and retreat at a moment's notice. The soldiers rode into battle with lances and swords, their expressions reflecting their determination.

The armor was a sight to behold, with intricate designs and patterns etched into bronze metal. The breastplates were adorned with serpents and mythical creatures, symbols of strength and power. The helmets were shaped like the heads of fierce warriors, with sharp ridges and crests. The shields were emblazoned with the Aryan emblem, a symbol of their unyielding power. The soldiers' weapons were equally impressive, with swords and spears crafted from the finest metals and adorned with precious gems.

"This is a force to be reckoned with," said a neighboring king, trembling with fear as he watched the Aryan army approach, their banners waving in the wind. "We cannot stand against them. Their military prowess is unmatched, their dominance unchallenged."

"You would do well to surrender now and spare your people the bloodshed," Indrasena said, his voice cold and unyielding, his words dripping with menace. "But if you resist, we will show no mercy. You will be brought before me to face justice, and your people will be subjugated."

The neighboring king hesitated, then accepted the defeat. "I surrender. Please, spare my people."

Indrasena smirked, his expression unyielding. "You have made a wise decision. Your people will be spared, but you will be brought before me to face justice."

And with that, the Aryan army marched on, their dominance unchallenged, their reputation for invincibility spreading far and wide.

* * *

But as they marched, a severe famine struck the Indus Valley region, brought on by a prolonged drought. The people suffered, their crops withering and dying, their rivers drying up. The once-green fields were now parched and barren, the skies gray and unforgiving. The people cried out to their gods for relief, but none came.

The Aryan army marched on, their weapons ready, but the people suffered, their eyes drowned with grief. The famine had taken a heavy toll.

In a small village, a family huddled together, their faces gaunt and weary. "How much longer can we endure this?" asked the wife, her voice barely above a whisper.

"I don't know," replied her husband, his eyes sunken with despair. "Our crops are dying, our rivers are dry. We've never seen a drought like this before."

"Our children are suffering. I don't know what to do. What have we done to anger the gods?" wife asked, her voice trembling.

Despite people's suffering, the Aryan army marched on, their dominance unchallenged, but the people's suffering was a stark reminder of the human cost of their conquests.

The Great Indus Valley Civilization, once a thriving and vibrant culture, was now in decline. The drought had ravaged the region, people were struggling to survive, and the population declined.

Families were scattered, their cities abandoned, and their culture was on the verge of being forgotten.

People were tired of the endless wars, the constant fear, and the suffering. They longed for a time when they could live without the threat of violence, when they could rebuild their cities and their lives. They prayed to their gods for an end to the bloodshed, for a chance to live in harmony once again.

* * *

The Aryan military prowess was unmatched, but a new influence was quietly spreading in the distant places. A philosophical movement, rooted in impermanence, non-self, and dependent origination, was taking root.

Its followers, scattered and unassuming, sought wisdom and liberation, rejecting the rigid social hierarchy and authority of the Varna system. This philosophy attracted adherents from all walks of life, offering a stark contrast to the empire's militaristic values.

As it spread, people began to engage with its principles and practices, discovering a new way of thinking that emphasized interconnectedness and impermanence. A new era of harmony and understanding seemed possible, but the alliance's dominant military culture resisted this change.

And at this crossroads of history, a single question echoed through the valley: would the allure of peace and wisdom be enough to overcome the entrenched power of war and tradition?

Chapter Twenty

The Rise of Buddhism

As the Aryan empire continued its expansion, a new spiritual movement began to emerge. Siddhartha Gautama, a wise and compassionate prince from the neighboring kingdom of Kapilavastu, had renounced his royal life to seek enlightenment.

Siddhartha was born into a life of luxury and privilege, the son of King Suddhodana and Queen Maya. He was raised in the palace, surrounded by wealth and opulence, and was trained in the arts of warfare and governance. But despite his privileged upbringing, Siddhartha was deeply troubled by the suffering he saw in the world.

"I seek answers to the suffering that plagues humanity," said Siddhartha, sitting under the Bodhi Tree. "I seek a path to inner peace, to non-violence, and to the rejection of material wealth."

And there, he discovered the Four Noble Truths, the Eightfold Path, and the concept of rebirth. Buddhism was born, a philosophy that emphasized inner peace, non-violence, and the rejection of material wealth. Its teachings resonated deeply with the people, offering a new way of living that was in harmony with the natural world and with each other.

The Four Noble Truths spoke directly to the hearts of those who sought a deeper understanding of life. They saw the Eightfold Path as a symbol of hope, a guide to living a life of compassion, wisdom, and inner peace.

Siddhartha, now known as the Buddha, was a tall and slender figure with a serene presence. His dark hair was short and curly, and his eyes were deep, piercing brown. He wore a simple robe, symbolizing his renunciation of worldly attachments. His gentle smile and compassionate gaze put those around him at ease, and his wisdom and understanding drew people to him like a magnet.

As his teachings spread, they attracted followers from all walks of life, including some within the Aryan empire. His message of non-violence, love, and wisdom resonated deeply, offering a stark contrast to the empire's militaristic values.

"This is a message of love and understanding," said one of his followers. "A message that resonates with the hearts of many."

"But what is the nature of this suffering?" asked another follower. "And how can we overcome it?"

"Suffering arises from our attachment to the ephemeral things of this world," replied Siddhartha. "It arises from our ignorance of the true nature of reality. But we can overcome it through the Eightfold Path, through the practice of mindfulness, compassion, and wisdom."

"And what of rebirth?" asked a third follower. "What happens to us when we die?"

"Our souls are reborn in a new body, a new life," said Siddhartha. "But we can break this cycle of rebirth through spiritual practice, through the attainment of enlightenment. We can achieve Nirvana, the state of ultimate peace and liberation.

But the Aryans were wary of this new culture. They saw it as a threat to their power, their dominance, and their very way of life.

"Buddhism is a weak and foreign influence," said Indrasena, the Aryan King. "It is unsuitable for the strong and proud Aryan people. We must forbid its practice within the empire."

"But, Indrasena, this is a philosophy of peace and compassion," argued one of his generals. "It teaches us to love and understand each other, to reject violence and conflict."

"I don't care for its teachings," replied Indrasena. "I care only for the strength and dominance of our empire. And Buddhism will weaken us, undermine our authority, and destroy our way of life."

And yet, Buddhism continued to spread, its message of love and understanding resonating with the hearts of many. A new conflict was brewing, one that would pit the Aryan empire against the peaceful followers of the Buddha. Tensions were rising between the two philosophical thoughts.

* * *

One day, a wise and compassionate figure appeared in the palace courtyard. It was Siddhartha Gautama, the Buddha, who had heard of Indrasena's tyranny and had come to offer guidance. Indrasena, intrigued by the monk's reputation, agreed to meet with him.

Indrasena stood tall and proud, his piercing gaze fixed on Siddhartha, the Buddha, who sat serenely on a low stone bench, his eyes closed in meditation.

"We will not be silenced," said a Buddhist monk, his eyes filled with determination.

"We will not be oppressed. We will continue to spread our message of love and understanding, no matter the cost."

Indrasena snarled; his face twisted in anger. "We will see how far you will go," he said. "We will crush this Buddhism, and we will maintain our dominance."

But Siddhartha remained calm, his eyes filled with compassion. "We do not seek conflict," he said. "We seek only to share our message of peace and love. Let us not be divided by our differences, but united by our common humanity."

Indrasena scoffed, his voice dripping with disdain. "You are naive, Siddhartha. Your words are empty, and your teachings are weak. We will not be swayed by your message of peace and love. We will continue to rule with strength and power."

Siddhartha's expression remained serene, his voice unwavering. "Strength and power may rule for a time, Indrasena, but they will never bring true peace or happiness. Only love and compassion can do that. And it is love and compassion that will ultimately triumph."

"The mind is everything, Indrasena," Siddhartha continued. "What you think, you become. Let go of your anger and hatred and embrace the present moment with kindness and understanding. Remember, the greatest victory is the victory over oneself."

Indrasena's face reddened with rage, but Siddhartha's words struck a chord deep within him. For a moment, he hesitated, and in that moment, a glimmer of understanding flashed in his eyes. But it was quickly extinguished by his pride and ambition.

The two men faced each other, Indrasena's gaze intense and unyielding, while Siddhartha's calm and peaceful demeanor seemed to radiate an aura of serenity. The fate of the Aryan empire and the future of Buddhism poised in uncertainty, as the winds of change blew fiercely around them.

The Aryan leader, however, saw this new movement as a threat to their power and dominance, and began to plot against the peaceful community of Buddhists.

Chapter Twenty-One

The Sacred Text

The Aryans, determined to counter the growing influence of Buddhism, sought to create a text that would reaffirm their values and beliefs. King Indrasena summoned the wisest minds in his kingdom to the palace, his eyes burning with urgency.

"We must respond to the Buddha's teachings," he declared. "Our people need a guiding light, a text that will remind them of their duty, honor, and courage." The scholars and sages nodded, their faces set with determination, and began their noble task.

And so, the Bhagavad-Gita was born. Written in the form of a dialogue between the warrior Arjuna and the divine Krishna, this sacred text wove together the threads of Aryan philosophy, spirituality, and martial tradition.

As the great war between the Pandavas and Kauravas raged on, Arjuna stood on the battlefield, his heart heavy with doubt. Before him lay the armies of his cousins, the Kauravas, and his own kin. He knew that, to fight would be to kill his own family, his own blood.

"What is my duty, Krishna?" asked Arjuna, his voice trembling with uncertainty.

"Your duty is to fight, Arjuna," replied Krishna. "To defend your people and uphold the natural order. You are a warrior, and this is your dharma."

"But Krishna, I am torn," said Arjuna. "I do not want to kill my own kin. Is there no other way?"

"There is no other way, Arjuna," said Krishna. "This war is just, and it is your duty to fight. But do not worry, for I will guide you. I will show you the path to spiritual growth and self-realization, even in the midst of war."

"But what of the cycle of rebirth?" asked Arjuna. "How can I escape the wheel of suffering?"

"The cycle of rebirth is broken through spiritual practice, Arjuna," said Krishna. "Through the practice of yoga, and the attainment of self-realization. You must focus on your duty and let go of attachment to the outcome."

"I see," said Arjuna. "I will do as you say, Krishna. I will fight, and I will seek spiritual growth."

"That is the spirit, Arjuna," said Krishna. "Remember, your duty is not just to fight, but to do so with honor and courage. And always remember, I am with you, guiding you on your path."

The Bhagavad-Gita extolled the virtues of duty, honor, and courage, emphasizing the importance of fulfilling one's role in society, even if it meant engaging in war and violence. It taught the concept of "Swadharma" - the idea that each individual has a unique role to play in the world, and that fulfilling that role is the key to spiritual growth.

As the Bhagavad-Gita spread throughout the region, people began to see a new path forward, one that honored their duties and roles in society while still seeking spiritual enlightenment. The text's message resonated deeply, offering a sense of purpose and belonging that resonated with the people of Indus Valley, reaffirming their values and beliefs, and cementing their commitment to their way of life.

And so, the two philosophies stood, like two great pillars, each one a monument to the power of human thought and spirituality. The Bhagavad-Gita and Buddhism, two different paths, each one guiding its followers towards enlightenment and understanding.

As the years passed, the Bhagavad-Gita's influence continued to grow, spreading beyond the borders of the Aryan empire and into the southern regions of the Deccan Plateau. It became a unifying force, bridging the cultural and linguistic divides between the Aryan north and the Dravidian south. The text's universal themes of spiritual growth, self-realization, and the quest for meaning transcended regional identities, speaking to people from all walks of life.

Chapter Twenty-Two

The Mahabharata:
A Household Name

The Bhagavad-Gita was just one part of a larger epic, the Mahabharata, which was now complete. This magnificent text, compiled by the sage Vyasa, told the story of the Pandavas and the Kauravas, two groups of cousins engaged in a great struggle.

"What is the purpose of this epic, Vyasa?" asked a disciple.

"The Mahabharata is a guide to living, a manual for humanity," replied Vyasa. "It teaches us about duty, family, loyalty, and power. It shows us the complexities of morality, ethics, and spirituality. But, my dear, it is more than that. It is a reflection of the human condition, a mirror held up to the soul."

"As I ponder the Mahabharata, I am struck by the cyclical nature of existence," said a philosopher. "The

Pandavas and the Kauravas, good and evil, light and darkness - are they not two sides of the same coin?"

"Indeed," replied Vyasa. "The Mahabharata teaches us that life is a never-ending cycle of birth, growth, decay, and rebirth. We are all caught in this cycle, struggling to find our place in the world."

"And what of free will?" asked another philosopher. "Do we truly have control over our actions, or are we bound by fate?"

"Ah, the age-old question," said Vyasa with a smile. "The Mahabharata shows us that our choices have consequences, but also that we are shaped by forces beyond our control. Perhaps the truth lies in the balance between free will and destiny."

As the Mahabharata spread throughout the land, it became a household name, a cultural touchstone that resonated with people from all walks of life. Its stories, characters, and teachings became an integral part of Aryan culture, shaping their values, beliefs, and traditions.

"The Mahabharata is a reminder that our actions have consequences, not just for ourselves, but for generations to come," said a wise elder.

"Indeed," replied Vyasa. "It teaches us to consider the impact of our actions on the world around us, to strive for dharma, for righteousness, and to cultivate compassion and wisdom."

The epic was recited and performed in temples, courts, and village squares, captivating audiences with its rich tapestry of heroes, villains, and divine beings. Its influence extended beyond literature, inspiring art, music, and even architecture.

"The Mahabharata is a living legacy of the power of storytelling," said a poet. "It reminds us that our stories shape us, that they contain the wisdom of our ancestors and the secrets of the world."

"Indeed," replied Vyasa. "The Mahabharata is a reminder that our stories are a part of us, that they contain the essence of our humanity. May we continue to tell them, to share them, and to learn from them."

The Mahabharata's impact was deep, cementing the Aryan identity and fostering a sense of shared heritage. It reminded them of their dharma, their values, and their place in the world. As the epic spread throughout the land, its influence reached every corner, consuming local traditions and even the remaining Harappan customs and practices. The Aryan customs and beliefs replaced the old ways, as the people embraced the new narrative and its teachings.

The Mahabharata became a cultural touchstone, shaping art, literature, and music. Its stories and characters inspired countless works of art, and its themes and motifs became the foundation for new literary and musical compositions. The epic's influence extended even to architecture, as temples and palaces were built to depict the gods and heroes of the Mahabharata.

The Harappan traditions, once a vibrant and thriving part of the people's identity, were all but forgotten, lost in the shadow of the Mahabharata's greatness.

And so, the Mahabharata remained, a hallmark of the power of storytelling and the enduring spirit of the Aryan people. Its influence will be felt for generations to come, shaping the culture of the subcontinent and the destiny of the people.

"May we walk the path of dharma," said a disciple.

"May we follow the teachings of the Mahabharata," replied Vyasa, his eyes filled with wisdom. "And may we always remember the wisdom of our ancestors, and the importance of our values."

Chapter Twenty-Three

The Buddhist Diaspora

As the Mahabharata's influence grew, Buddhist monks began to feel increasingly unwelcome in the Aryan empire. They saw the text's emphasis on duty, honor, and power as contradictory to the Buddha's teachings of compassion, non-violence, and spiritual liberation.

"We are forced to leave our homeland, our temples, and our people," said a Buddhist monk, his voice heavy with the feeling of separation.

"The Mahabharata preaches the story of war and violence," said another monk, his eyes filled with tears. "How can we remain in a land that glorifies the conquest?"

As the Mahabharata's influence grew, Buddhist monks found themselves unwelcome in their own temples. They were met with cold stares and hostile whispers, their teachings dismissed as "foreign" and "subversive." One by one, they packed their belongings and slipped away, seeking refuge in distant lands.

They migrated to Tibet, China, Japan, and other places, carrying with them the sacred texts, teachings, and traditions of Buddhism.

"We leave behind our loved ones, our friends, and our community," said a monk, his voice cracking. "We are forced to start anew, in a foreign land, with only our faith to guide us."

In Tibet, they found a fertile ground for their teachings, and Buddhism flourished, becoming an integral part of Tibetan culture. In China, they encountered Taoist and Confucian traditions, and a rich cultural fusion emerged. In Japan, they introduced Zen Buddhism, which resonated deeply with the Samurai warriors.

A monk's eyes would cloud over, remembering the scent of sandalwood and incense wafting through the temples they once called home. Another would finger the worn wooden beads of his mala, recalling the gentle touch of his teacher's hand. In the silence of their new surroundings, they heard the echoes of their past, the memories of loved ones left behind.

"We have gained a new home, but we have lost our roots," said a monk, his voice filled with nostalgia.

"We are like trees planted in foreign soil, struggling to thrive."

As Buddhism spread across the known world, it transformed cultures, inspired art and literature, and nurtured spiritual seekers. But for the monks, it was a bittersweet victory.

"May we walk the path of the Buddha," said a monk, his voice barely above a whisper.

"May we follow the teachings of compassion, non-violence, and spiritual liberation," replied another monk, his eyes filled with tranquility.

As they lit the evening lamps, a monk's gaze would drift to the flickering flame, his thoughts carried back to the temples they had left behind. He would whisper a silent prayer, his voice barely audible, "May the light of our ancestors guide us, and may we never forget the paths we walked, and the hearts we loved."

Chapter Twenty-Four

The Universal God

As the Mahabharata's influence continued to spread, Krishna's status as a divine being grew. He was no longer just a revered figure in the Aryan empire, but a universal God, worshipped and revered across the land.

"Krishna's teachings transcend time and space," said a philosopher. "They speak to the human condition, to our deepest hopes and fears. His message of love and compassion is a reminder that we are not alone in this vast universe, that we are connected to something greater than ourselves."

His teachings, as recorded in the Bhagavad-Gita, were seen as timeless wisdom, applicable to all people, regardless of their background or beliefs.

His message of love, compassion, and selfless action resonated deeply with the human heart, speaking to the universal longing for meaning and purpose.

"Krishna's divinity is not limited to one religion or creed," said a mystic. "He is the embodiment of the ultimate reality, the unchanging essence that underlies all existence. His teachings are a reminder that we are not separate, that we are all part of the same divine whole."

A Buddhist monk, a Jain scholar, and a Hindu priest stood together, united in their devotion to Krishna. "Though our paths may differ," they said, "we recognize the same divine love and guidance in his teachings."

* * *

As the years passed, the Aryan kingdom, once a unified and powerful force, began to fracture and splinter. The vast empire was divided into smaller kingdoms, each ruled by a different king. The unity and cohesion that had defined the Aryan kingdom under Indrasena's leadership began to unravel, as petty squabbles and regional interests took precedence over the greater good.

Ashoka, a young prince with a fierce determination in his heart, emerged as a beacon of hope. He traveled from kingdom to kingdom, meeting with rulers and diplomats, forging alliances and negotiating treaties. His charisma and vision inspired others to follow him, and soon, a new empire began to take shape.

Ashoka's reign was marked by peace and prosperity. He encouraged trade and commerce, and the arts and culture flourished once more. He built new roads, planted trees, and his people prospered. But as the years went by, his successors began to squabble and fight among themselves, and the empire began to fracture once more.

The cycle of time repeated itself, as empires rose and fell, and new leaders emerged to forge their own paths. And yet, amidst the ruins of a bygone era, a glimmer of hope remained – the knowledge that the power of love and compassion could always bring people together, and that the legacy of Krishna's teachings would endure forever.

Chapter Twenty-Five

The Dawn of a New Era

As the worship of Krishna continued to flourish, a new philosophical thought, known as the Bhakti movement, emerged. This faith emphasized the power of personal devotion, love for the divine, and defied the rigid social hierarchies and varna system.

"The divine is within us, and our love is the bridge to connect with it," said Meerabai, a charismatic devotee.

"The teachings of Hinduism and Buddhism have shown us the way to inner peace and spiritual freedom," said Ramakrishna, a wise sage. "We have learned to embrace love and compassion as the highest virtues, and to see the divine in everyone."

The teachings resonated deeply with the people, who were drawn to its message of inclusivity, compassion, and spiritual freedom. Charismatic

Sadhus and poets traveled the land, sharing their vision of a loving and merciful God.

"The divine is not just a distant concept, but a living presence in our hearts," said Kabir, a poet. "We feel its presence in every moment, in every breath. And this presence is what unites us all, beyond our external differences."

As this new faith spread, it drew people from various backgrounds, including Buddhism, Jainism, and Hinduism. Its inclusive nature and focus on love and compassion created a sense of unity and shared purpose among its followers.

"Hinduism has taught us the importance of spiritual exploration and self-inquiry," said Ramakrishna. "Buddhism has shown us the path to inner peace and enlightenment. We have learned from both traditions and incorporated their wisdom into our faith."

"In the end, it was not the doctrines or dogmas that mattered, but the love that flowed from the heart," said Meerabai. "For in the depths of that love, lies the true essence of the divine, and the unity that binds us all."

"May we continue to learn from each other's traditions and wisdom," said Ramakrishna. "May our love for the divine be the guiding light that illuminates our path, and may we always remember the unity and shared humanity that binds us all."

"The world is a garden, and love is the flower that blooms in it," said Ramakrishna. "Let us nurture this flower, and let its beauty and fragrance fill our lives and our world."

"And so, let us embrace this love, and let it guide us towards a world of compassion, unity, and spiritual freedom. For in this love, we find the true meaning of our existence, and the key to a brighter future for all humanity."

The End